Black

Sheep

Boy

a novel-in-stories

Black
Martin
Sheep
Pousson
Boy

Barnacle | Rare Bird
Los Angeles, Calif.

This is a Genuine Barnacle Book

A Barnacle Book | Rare Bird Books
453 South Spring Street, Suite 302
Los Angeles, CA 90013
rarebirdbooks.com

Set in Cochin
Printed in the United States

10 9 8 7 6 5 4 3 2 1

Publisher's Cataloging-in-Publication data

Names: Pousson, Martin, author.

Title: Black sheep boy : a novel in stories / by Martin Pousson.

Description: First Hardcover Edition | A Barnacle Book | Los Angeles
[California] , New York [New York] : Rare Bird Books, 2016.

Identifiers: ISBN 978-1-942600-37-4.
Subjects: LCSH Gays—Fiction | Bayous—Fiction. | Louisiana—Fiction.
| Bildungsroman. | Family—Fiction. | Cajuns—Fiction. | Magic realism
(Literature). | BISAC FICTION/Literary.
Classification: LCC PS3616.O87 .B43 | DDC 813.6—dc23

For Odd Ducks, Strange Birds, and Queer Fish

TABLE OF CONTENTS

I.

II.

I.

TALES OF THE *DÉRANGEMENT*

"In response to Le Grand Dérangement, their mass exile and exodus from L'Acadie by the British, the Acadians began to sing sad songs of upheaval and loss but also strange songs of frogs and other creatures. These songs confused Les Américains, and that was part of the point."

— Beausoleil Canard,
Cajuns: Three Countries, Two Continents
& One Weird Trunk

"*Saute, crapaud, ta queue va bruler;*
Mais prends courage, elle va repousser!"

"Jump, frog, your tail will burn;
But take heart, it will return!"

—"Saute Crapaud"
Columbus "Boy" Frugé

FOREWORD

NIGHT SONG

At the end of the long hot day, the wires snapped overhead, the power dropped in the house, and the air conditioner died again. Through the open window, bayou fog wound around my neck like a cottonmouth snake, with its breath of wet smoke. Cradled against my mother's side, my wild head of hair rained sweat down my arm to a pair of twitching hands. The sweat bonded my mother to me as I looked to her face for a sign of recognition. We lay in her bed with a hurricane lantern, my left side propped up by her arm as her steady finger moved across the page of a book, tracing the black lines, the marks she called words. Out loud, she read each sentence with added stress, her face a dramatic mask of sound.

They haunted me, my mother and that book. *The Blown-Around Room* starred a white-cheeked boy who, in just a few pages, turned red as a crawfish. He'd been ordered to straighten his bedroom, but the pictures revealed him sleeping instead of cleaning. Or else throwing a ball at an imaginary basket until it bounced to the side and overturned all the boxes in his closet. Suddenly, everything that should've been hidden, everything that belonged in drawers or on shelves was sitting like an angry squall in the middle of his room, out in the open for anyone to see. At the sound of the crash, his mother pried open the door and—before her vigilant eye—he turned into a little monster. Red in the face with a wild bush of hair on his head, he no longer resembled the cherub of the opening. There was only one word for what he'd become at that point, and my mother called it out loud: "Devil!"

When her wide eyes turned to me, I knew what to do: I repeated the word and looked for her recognition. She nodded, letting me know that I got it right, then pointed again to the stormy face of the boy and the disaster that surrounded him.

"See," she said, "see what can happen."

In her view, every story had to have a point. She wanted to know the outcome, so she sometimes read the last page first, letting its revelation ring throughout the whole tale.

"Of course, he had to turn into a devil," she declared, "for it said so in the end."

At that, she clicked her tongue with vindication. The blown-around boy was locked in the tale by my mother, who was now the author, and I was his shadow.

I would make a mess of things too. I would knock over boxes meant to be shut, stumble over a tangle of clothes on the floor, fall down with a red face and a flaming bush of hair. The whole book—every word—was a sign of what would happen, of the horror ahead.

1.

REVIVAL GIRL

Under the fluorescent glare of the kitchen, Mama sang a gospel tune and shelved groceries to an imaginary beat. Each can, bottle, and box faced forward, like votive offerings. Lined in straight rows, the pantry rack collected a religious order, only missing gold leaf and stained glass. Food was hallowed in Louisiana, its magic put to work in all manner of faiths. Not just herbs for hexes but roots, leaves, seeds, bones, and skins. Spells, cures, omens, all called for some piece of a plant or part of an animal that might also land on a dinner plate. If you wanted to quell the nerves, you stuffed a bag with the hairy flower of frog-foot. If you wanted to hinder the heart, you stewed the hooked fruit of devil's claw. And if you wanted to predict the sex of a baby, you swung a meaty tailbone over the pregnant belly. A steady swing meant a boy, a gyrating swing meant a girl, and an in-between swing meant a third kind of baby, the kind no one wanted to name.

There I stood in Mama's tall shadow, the no-name kind of baby. The light from the fridge radiated a halo around her dark cloud of hair. A carton of eggs glowed in her hand. Her long legs shifted back and forth, like a crane at dawn. Even though she tapped her heels to the song, I knew better than to tap along with her or, worse, to twirl across the linoleum flapping my hands in the air. By three, I'd learned penance for the jitters when Mama strapped down my restless hands with duct tape then ordered a doctor to fit braces on my twisting feet. By five, I'd learned sacrifice for the stutters when another doctor cut out a flap of flesh to correct my tangling speech. Mama showed me the horn-shaped piece to prove a point: the devil had me by the tongue. So I did my best to walk straight and talk steady.

Still, my feet pranced and my arms swung more than any boy Mama had known. At first glance, my body seemed drawn into the right shape, but my walk swished and swayed, and my hands flapped in the air or flitted at my side. A tremor in my chest pushed my ribs out when I grew anxious, as if I might burst. At times, I stared at a point between my eyes before boxing my ears with two fists or slapping my face with an open palm. Just what brewed inside me? Mama wondered. Just what made up my tailbone? Soon, she'd open that carton of eggs in her hand. Soon, she'd test that boy on the floor.

Cousins, blood relations, were the only boys Mama had known before marrying at sixteen. Short boys smelling of foul ditches, with loose tongues, rough hands, stiff lips, headed for the half-life of the oil patch. And the only man she knew, her towering father, had gone by the time she hit her teens, leaving her to tend two baby sisters and, as she put it, a baby mother. The girls made monstrous faces from the floor, crying for milk, syrup, toys, solace.

Her mother, my *mamère*, was an angry baby too, full grown, with three daughters and half a husband, but prone to pouting for days on end and pulling at her face until marks and stains rose on her skin. Jaundiced, with an odd yellow cast and a flame-red mark near her left eye, she frowned and winced and usually wore what the frosted-wig Cajun ladies called *le grimace*.

"That woman is marked," they said, while rubbing their hands over a set of rosary beads. As soon as they heard she was from Sulphur, they knew the cause. That place looked, smelled, and tasted yellow. Water streamed with colored bits, soil crumbled into colored chunks, and air choked with colored clouds. Oil derricks clotted the town like metal birds boring for food. Tanker trucks rocked the roads leaving a tail of exhaust fumes and a crest of mineral traces. Who could look at all that and see anything but the devil?

Mama had heard the legends about her mother's town and her father's cove, where Sabine men dug into the swampy ground with their own homemade drills and bits to raise houses on piers. Or else they pushed off the land altogether to float in house boats on the Vermilion or the Teche, the phantom limbs of the Mississippi. Any oil drilled out of the ground, any minerals pumped into the air, didn't belong to them. They owned no land, only boats, no farms, only fishing nets. And they did their best to outrun the changing tides and shifting coast of the gulf.

A girl in that place was her own dowry. With sable-black hair and a body that swayed like a cattail reed, Mama could've had any Sabine man. The center of her irises flashed a speckled green and her skin flushed with a copper flame. She was true Cajun on one side, *la vraie chose*, but Sabine on the other, an odd mix of French, African, and a dying Indian tribe. The wolf-faced boys opened their mouths in a howl when she passed. But she wanted no half-life, no half-husband, no near-man. She wanted no floating home. So she sang to herself and waited for a boy from another town and the exit sign.

And what had she learned before she left the cove, before she married? That the devil lurked everywhere, in drinking water, in mud under your shoe, in the wrath and cholera of family. That faith had to be conjured, cooked up with a powerful hand. That women snapped at each other like crawfish in a boiling pot while men ran like horses through wide open fields.

Her father had galloped in and out the front door for years, sometimes with another woman at his side. He reared back, dropped her on the couch, then hollered into the kitchen for a tall girl. He laughed at his own joke, calling his tall daughter to bring him a tall can of beer. Mama got the joke but didn't laugh. She worried how he magically pulled a six-pack from a paper sack while she rationed lost bread for her sisters, spiked off milk with syrup, and shaved slices from the block of gray cheese. Yet if the bread, the milk, the cheese, and—yes—the beer rankled, her father's women impressed Mama with their light hair and light eyes and elevated him above their lot.

He was elevated in other ways too. As part-time minister in the church of the Pentecost, and as full-time voodoo *traiteur,* my *papère* soared even before his crane of a daughter. In a tent revival, he stood head and shoulders above the penitents when he walked the aisles waving the Holy Bible. He leaned over weeping women and called foreign words out of their mouth. He shouted down stooping men and pulled ailments out of their body. Throughout, he smiled wide, his forehead glistened, and even the fillings in his teeth gleamed in testament to his word. Then at home, he raised his hand to the porch ceiling to hang black chickens, their guts dripping like yellow rain. From his seat on a wingback chair, he cured a baby's deadly whooping cough with a rabbit's belly and the milky sap of a tala tree. He ground up stinging nettle to make a gullet-scorching brew for a man who cheated him in cards. He burned onion skins for money and peanut shells for luck. He rubbed his hairy hand over a doll with a worried cross-stitched mouth while Mama's cousins collected at his feet and called him Chief.

Her father could work magic both ways, the white voodoo and the black. The rumor was, given some moolah, a shot, and a pair of dice, he could solve any predicament. He'd throw the numbers on the ground, slam the shot down his throat, then strut around like a rooster with his tail on fire until he finally slapped his hands together and shouted, "Sweet Jesus!"

And, like that, he could tell you in exactly what part of the woods to find a thirty-point buck or how to exhume a dead skunk from under your house with nothing but a chain of beer tabs, a fish hook, and a free hand. He knew from whose backyard to steal the best sassafras root, which herbs needed rubbing together to cure a child's croup, and how to boil chicken gizzards and bayou gum to induce an immobilizing pox or a severe case of the runs for whoever dared to cross you.

With shoulder-length hair, a hawk-like nose, and a chin so sharp it could work as a nutcracker, in her stories Mama's father was the one man who could hold the entire world, steady and straight. Once, he spun an egg in his hand before her very eyes without it ever falling or hitting the ground. With a single tap, the whole shell fell away like brittle candy and there stood the perfect egg.

Yet she also saw her father crack. She watched him heat up a spoon with black tar before sticking a needle into his skin. Or else he rolled up tin foil and stuck a straw in a line of smoke. Soon she smelled it—the sulfur in the air—and with that whiff, she knew he'd become the other man. He might, with a single horse kick, put a hole through the bedroom door. He might run outside and send a fruit tree sailing through the front window. He might tear the whole house in two.

Just before she turned thirteen, Mama saw her father lifted in his wingback chair by a sheriff and two deputies. He refused to budge when they showed a summons, so they carried that chair off the porch and onto the lawn where they dumped him into a net. He let loose a howl as they slapped a pair of handcuffs on his wrist then laughed and shouted a streak of hot words in French. Her mother emerged from the bedroom, suddenly an old lemon-faced woman, crying that she had married a werewolf, while women in wigs stood at the edge of the ditch, clucking their tongues. The red lights flashed and the siren shrieked as they drove her father away.

Yet they couldn't drive him out of her mind. Her eyes saw him everywhere: in passing cars, in big-armed trees, in a waking dream. He stood onstage under a tent wide as a sugar cane field. His feet floated above the ground and his hand reached out to heal a congregation of writhing people all at once. A young girl sang at his back, a raucous number that made the tent shake from side to side. He slapped his hand on the Bible then turned up a palm with an egg in the center, a brilliant white. Then the dream flickered and went dark on a single dancing flame.

Within weeks, she found a tent, filled with rolling bodies and a tall minister hoisting the Good Book overhead. A girl was pulled onstage to sing lead on a gospel song. When the words left her mouth, the tent billowed and the poles buckled. "He's got the whole world in His hands," she sang, as if each syllable were followed by an exclamation mark. People lifted their heads to the sky, shook their lips open until words tore out, and yanked their own hair until their scalps bled. Those with shoes tossed them onto the stage and joined those without. Together, they dug their feet into the muddy soil making a greasy floor. In the middle of all that grease, they danced faster and faster, more and more furiously, sawing their legs in and out to the beat of the gospel song. Some ripped at a sleeve or a collar, others were left standing in their underwear before the minister shouted a foreign word and promised to drop them in the water. When she caught his eye, though, she saw a ring of yellow and knew his magic was phony. His smile was too tight, his forehead too dry, and his hands too small. That minister had none of her father's power, none of his fire or faith. No man did. Not any minister anywhere, not one of her cousins or uncles then, and not her husband now.

When she made her move out of the dark roux of the swamp, Mama headed for the light grain of the rice field. She traded the Pentecostal faith for the Catholic one. She donned a mantilla and gloves, gave up the week-long revivals, the robed choir, the stamping feet and overturned chairs, and even the language of tongues—all for a man with a job in another town and a car to drive her away. To her, away meant another world. It meant a new life. It meant the promise of anywhere but here.

Even so, she made a gumbo faith, a jambalaya religion. During Mass, she wondered at the mortification of the saints, the bloody Crucifixion of Christ, and the seven swords in the Mother of Sorrows. She endured the boredom of the liturgy and the drone of the homily. Yet at home, she turned on the AM radio to hear the storm of a gospel song break out in her ears, a chorus of voices rising in a ferocious wind, lifting her higher and higher, on a soaring bird, a galloping horse, carrying her further and further away.

The man she married—my father—had a dry forehead, like that phony minister, she said. Small hands and a small quiet chest too. He'd taken her no more than half an hour from the bayou cove and gave her no more than half a house. A duplex apartment with plastic counters, plastic floors, and plastic lights overhead. It was brick, she had to admit, not cinder block. And the walls weren't stuffed with *bousillage*. But still she wanted out.

Her mind rattled with maps and compasses and a spinning wheel of direction. Her ears echoed with the hum of old women and old stories. Her eyes burned with flaming creatures and the yellow sign of a dead-end. And now in the altar of the kitchen, she wanted to know: could I deliver? Could I direct her out of here?

Mama raised her hand to testify, playing minister, choir, and congregation all at once. She sang louder and higher than the radio, her voice rocking the air around us until it shook like a thunder cloud. Half the words drowned under the raining clap of her hands, while the other half tore out in a lightning flash.

"You and me, brother, in His hands!"

Clap, clap!

"You and me, sister, in His hands!"

Clap, clap!

At the end of each verse, she twirled around to stare at me on the floor, checking to see if I was still there or if I'd tipped over into a place she couldn't reach. While she sang, her long finger pointed down at my head then made jabs in the air around her. I followed that finger and must've struggled to figure out the meaning of her dance. Each wave of her arm, each blink of her eye, each clap of her hands revealed another mystery, dark and cryptic. Soon something would crack. I'd move my mouth, my arms, or my legs in the wrong way. Soon, I'd end up in sitting in another doctor's office or kneeling on the kitchen floor with hands taped to my chest.

Instead, Mama opened the carton of eggs, took one out and placed it in my hand. She looked straight into my eyes, as if she could see affirmation, a prayer or votive. Then she balanced the egg in the middle of my palm, upside down on its northern point and — for a long moment — it spun in a perfect orbit.

In the Golden Book stories Mama read at night, the cherubic altar boy would've carried that egg—proud and high, sure and steady—like an alabaster tooth from the mouth of God. But the devil boy would've bared his own yellow teeth, would've shaken the egg and sucked the yolk right out of the shell. What was I, Mama wanted to know, cherub or devil? What was I, a steady boy or another kind?

"Hold it," she said, "hold it."

Her eyes grew wide and glowed like green marbles. Here was her hope. Here was her way out of this cramped house, with its bell jar rooms and matchbox furniture. Here was her toddler listening to her command. She'd done right to read proper English to me, to forbid anyone to speak Cajun gibberish over my crib. She'd done right to show me how to genuflect, how to bow, how to button a shirt, how to clean under my nails, how to stay out of the sun, how to keep my face white, how to be a real man, not a wild little Sabine beast.

"Hold it," she said, "hold it."

It was a whole world, that egg. Now it spun in my hand. And as long as Mama gazed at me, it kept spinning. Before her magic-making eyes, I became the cherub and performed another wondrous miracle. Her baby who walked before his first birthday and talked before he walked, her boy who lined up all his toys in straight rows, her son who just the night before sat upright in his bed sleep-talking from Holy Scripture, this son of hers was now carrying the world she placed in his hands.

He was now performing the same magic as her lost father, that minister and traiteur.

"Hold it," she said, "Hold it as long as you can."

Then before her eyes and mine, the egg began to spin out of control in a shaky orbit. It was a simple command, just a couple of words, but I couldn't get it right, couldn't keep it straight. I should've known how to hold it, like her folklore father, how to control the world she gave me. But the wobbly sphere in my hand turned round and round, and my eyes crossed as it spun faster and faster, more and more furiously until it looked like a storm in my palm, the tiny white eye of a hurricane.

Then my fingers twitched, my palm shook, a storm broke out, and the whole world went spinning. The egg flew from my hand to the floor, setting off a display of yolky lightning along the way. Mama's newly mopped floor, the bleached tiles, the white cabinets, her gleaming patent leather shoes, and the trim of her skirt were all coated in yellow sticky ooze. Though I'd dropped only one egg, it looked as if a dozen brilliant suns had burst all around us. I stared at Mama, and she stared at me, until the nerves in my legs began to buckle. I slapped down my palm, trying to numb the pulsing sensation. But when Mama's long finger pointed at me, a warm, yellow trickle ran down my leg and collected in a puddle at my bare feet. In a flash, I plunged my hands down my pants to squeeze off the problem.

And that's when it all finally cracked. Mama took a good hard look at me and suddenly saw the devil before her. She'd somehow missed it all along, how she'd given birth not to a perfect Cajun son, not to a Catholic altar boy, but to bayou spawn, a pant-wetting, egg-dropping son of Satan.

"What in the Hell!" she kept screaming, her eyes wide and wild. "What in the sulfur-reeking, flame-licking, burning name of Hell are you doing with your hands in your pants?"

"Holding it," I said.

"Holding it!" she screamed.

My answer and her echo sent Mama running for the fridge. When she turned back around, she glowed the way she would in a dream, and I could no longer say what was true and what was not. I had dropped an egg. That much was certain. I had broken my mother's heart with a weak small hand. That was certain too. Yet was she singing that song? Was she clapping like mad?

When I looked up, Mama had turned into a red-eyed furious little girl staring down a jittery phantom. In one hand she held the carton of eggs, with the lid flipped open, and in the other she was cradling a phosphorescent white oval in her palm. She didn't place this one in my hand, though. Instead, she flung it to the ground. Then she flung another egg at the cabinet. Suddenly eggs were flying everywhere—at the sink, the stove, the baseboard. At the walls, the floor, the countertop. Mostly, though, at me. Egg ran down my face and arms and into my mouth before the carton was empty, the kitchen was coated yellow, and she finally stopped.

Tears ran down Mama's dream face in little rivers, then they ran down mine too. Along with the eggs, my mouth became a sea of grainy salt and slimy sulfur.

Yet the revival wasn't over. Mama dragged me across the kitchen to the concrete floor of the pantry where she planted me on two skinny knees. Lord knows her son had made a mess. Lord knows how badly she wanted me to get it right, to be the good cherub. And *everyone* knows a revival's not over until someone is stricken by the spirit, accused of some unholy crime, and made to confess. Eyes cross, tongues thicken, and whole bodies go rolling into the aisle. I kneeled and begged forgiveness, while a string of Blessed Be's and Hallowed Names crossed my mother's lips and she chased herself around the room, shouting as if her hair had been singed and her feet were on fire.

Finally, she dragged me to the closet in my bedroom and shut the door. Between the slats, I could see her tall slim figure pacing back and forth in front of my bed. And before her shadow slipped out of view, I heard one voice, then two, rising high and loud, singing the song from the kitchen and clapping to the beat of a pair of heels.

"You and me, brother, in His hands!"

Clap, clap!

"You and me, sister, in His hands!"

Clap, clap!

In the darkness, I bit my arm until I raised a red bump. I bit long and hard until I could no longer hear the sound of those two divided voices. The falling voice of a woman dropping something precious from her hand, and the rising voice of a girl watching in horror as it hit the ground. The low raging thunder of the words, and the high crying rain of the song.

"The itty bitty baby in His hands!"

"He's got the whole world in His hands!"

Oh, but where are the soaring horses now, Mama? Where are all the men? Who will be there when the storm breaks, when the hand drops, when the Pentecost falls?

2.

WANTED MAN

In the ray of light just outside the bathroom door, I waited for my father's resurrection. When he got home from the battle of work, he looked dead as a blind buck in the road. The only signs of life were foreboding. His eyes were bloodshot and bulging veins snaked down his neck. One eye twitched and both hands trembled. With a jutting chin and twisted grin, Papa looked like a black and white poster for a wanted man, a legend everyone passes but no one sees.

At five, I'd already begun to mourn my father. His arms had held me once, his gruff beard rubbed against my face. His lips pressed against my belly, my nose, my eyes. He carried me on his back so that I towered over the house or he carried me on his side, so that—as he put it—his son could see everything his way. Cradled against him, I felt the warm and quickening beat inside his chest. Yet he no longer lifted me up, and his hands hardly ever laid on top of my head now. So I followed as he cut new tracks in the St. Augustine lawn, I raced as he headed for the garage, and I scouted souvenirs from his path: shiny beer bottle caps and glossy gum wrappers. Wherever he went, I lurked in his footsteps and shadowed his trail, in the hope of spying a glimmer of the father I wanted to know.

At seventeen, he was a local football star outrunning other boys on the field not with brute strength but with wily dodges and sneaky plays. At eighteen, he was a married man holding a son instead of a trophy, a ball, or a diploma. In name at least, he was head of a household. But where other men might've seen a new field to maneuver and dominate, Papa saw rising water and vanishing turf. He struggled to stay afloat with bills, taxes, and his wife's teary tirades. His ears nearly drowned with her demands for more space, a bigger car, a faster way to a new home in a new neighborhood. New curtains, new carpet, new wallpaper. What he couldn't afford, he charged. Still, she cried out that she was stuck or suffocated or stifled. If he touched her, she flinched. If he kissed her, she shivered. If he raised his voice or stamped his foot, she blanched and broke into tears.

Whatever man Mama wanted, he bore another face at home, wore another shirt at work. Rather than outrun that man, Papa camouflaged himself and stepped lightly over the threshold every day. He moved like a chastened animal or a man whose hands might get him into trouble. Arms at his side, eyes still and straight, and blond hair turned to early ash, he approached even his son with caution. Gingerly, he pushed pin into cloth, changing my diapers as if they were silk, as if I was a sleeping butterfly. Warily, he pushed a spoon into my mouth, feeding me from glass jars as if I too might shatter and break. He coddled me so much, so often, and so completely, that neighbors started to talk. Their chatter rose loud enough to reach even his drowned ears. What was happening in that flip-flop house? What did it mean when a man mothered, yes, mothered a child? If we'd been Greek, a chorus would've mounted the stage with urgent warnings and dire prophecies. Reversal means tragedy, and tragedy means someone will fall. And that someone, no doubt, would be me.

We weren't Greek, of course, we were Cajun. Still, the drama persisted. And with Papa cast in the role of mother, Mama saw no choice but to wear another costume, to pull on boots and lay down rules. Before she lit the fifth candle on my cake, she issued her proclamation: no baby talk, no Cajun *ya ya*, no childish nursery rhymes, and no more holding, touching, or kissing. *She* would feed their son, *she* would bathe him, and *she* would tell him stories at night. Period. After all, his baby was meant to be her little man, her bright Cajun prince.

Yet she was too late. The light had long gone out on Cajun men in Louisiana, not because of any woman, but because they were—day by day—losing their religion. Not the religion of the Catholic church, which seemed filled with priests scheming for ways to run their fingers under the hem of an altar boy's skirt. Not the religion of the Cajun language, which no one had even bothered to write down and which already had lost all currency. Not the religion of love, which left them nothing but confused. Not even the religion of the bottle, which never left their side. No, the biggest religion wasn't practiced or preached, wasn't spoken or sipped. It was played.

Cajun musicians were worshipped like demigods in Acadiana. Before he married any woman, a Cajun man served as a high priest in a chank-a-chank church. Along with a gang of cousins and *fatras*, he might've led a band. At the very least, he could clang a triangle or bang a cowbell. Besides having the Eucharist in his blood, every Cajun also had an accordion, a fiddle, a tit-fer, and a musical washboard. Until my grandfather's time, every man could drain a six-pack in five-minutes flat and make a fiddle cry like a cat at a crawfish boil. After the American schools opened on the Cajun prairie, though, my grandfather became the first man in his family to master the English language and the last to hear his own father play the squeezebox.

By the time he was old enough to work, there was no money in Cajun music — or Cajun anything. So he let his father's accordion lay silent and never picked up a bow or fiddle. With his English, he worked for a surveyor. With his wages, he bought a piece of land and stepped behind the wheel of a plow. If my grandfather couldn't hold up the full moon of a Eucharist like a Catholic priest or saw a fiddle in half like his uncles, then there was only one thing left for his hands to do. He'd dig deep into the ground and pull up long stalks of Louisiana short grain. He'd rub the rice hull with his thumb until the brown turned gold. He'd stay out in the fields until darkness fell and the last church bell tolled.

While the men walked away from their chank-a-chank religion, the Cajun women walked the Stations of the Cross. At church, they rubbed rosary beads with holy fury. At home, they scrubbed wood floors with holy force. Who'd blame them for praying so fervently to hold the house together? Who'd blame them for scouring so frantically? Without the mantilla-headed women, their husbands and sons might've all grown long tails and disappeared into the swamp.

After all, women were the last keepers of the living faith. What was left of Acadiana was threaded on their looms, in their cross-stitching and in the fabric of their gossip. According to them, farming rice was the only honest work left for a Cajun man. With her own Good Book, my grandmother proclaimed sugar cane farmers "decadent," shrimpers "low-lifes," and oil men "nothing but the tobacco juice of the devil." She had other sayings too, as many as there were numbers in Deuteronomy or names in Numbers.

"Hush my mouth," to any piece of gossip she intended to pass on.

"Higher than a cat's back," to any price she refused to pay.

And "God don't like ugly," to any man, woman, or child who dared disagree with her.

She might've also said "God don't like dirty" for all the force she put into bleaching already-white walls and scrubbing already-clean floors. Like a good Catholic penitent, my grandmother fell on her hands and knees before God and before the evil menace of dirt. All that bleach and ammonia must've filled her head with fumes, as Papa put it, for soon she started wearing latex gloves at the dinner table and foam slippers in bed. She ordered her husband to drop his farm boots at the door but still chased his footsteps with a broom. Perhaps my grandmother had forgotten that rice was not only a seed, not only a grain, but also a germ. And a dusty one at that. Rice husk clung to my grandfather's clothes and heels like a combustible line of ash. One short fuse and he might've blown up.

Instead, he broke down. With all his wife's constant talk of dirt and the devil, with all her plastic-wrapped fingers and toes following him to bed, and with all the sad lost music in his head, my grandfather's nerves finally snapped. He hollered at every object in the house: the rug that tripped, the clock that lied, the chair that chattered, the desk that bruised, and the broom that chased. He seemed to have lost all sense of place in the house, stopping to scrutinize a hallway or looking around a corner with a suspicious eye before taking a step forward. Soon, lead collected in his feet, then in both his hands. Maybe the rice in the field would rot, maybe snakes would take over the garden, maybe frogs would clot up the windows, and maybe birds would fall out of the sky and hit the roof, but he refused to budge until my grandmother called the rectory and two men in gowns dribbled oil on his forehead, muttered prayers, and rubbed beads. One led the rosary, the other read gospels from the Holy Bible. Both sipped from a bottle and ate plate after plate delivered from the kitchen. They left with a fat church envelope while my grandfather remained silent and still in bed. In the morning, though, there was a pool of oily vomit and a depression on the pillow where his head had rested. A low wheezing sound filled the air, like an accordion played with a deep reed and heavy bellows. The room smelled of camphor and dead leaves and my grandfather was not ever seen in any one of the twenty-two parishes of Acadiana again.

That's when my father set out to find a woman who'd be the opposite of my grandmother. At first, Mama must've seemed as unlike a Catholic housewife as a girl in Louisiana could get. No frosted wig, no powdered face, no mantilla on her head. Instead, she had hair the color of motor oil and skin as dark and smooth as tawny leather. When she sat in his car, he wanted to drive like a madman through fields of sugar cane and rows of sweet potatoes, over gravel and shell and smack into the only stop sign in town.

Yet if my father thought a Pentecostal, revival-singing daughter of a voodoo man would be fond of dirt and rice chaff, if he thought she would sit idly by in the passenger seat, he was as wrong as a right hand turn in a cul-de-sac road. That turn might've landed him in the driveway of his own home, but the woman inside and the house itself were on fire with sanitizing fumes.

As soon as he got back from work, Papa followed Mama's finger to the bathroom. He'd tried to plot a path away from his parents' home, but he ended up right where he damn well started. He'd taken a step out of my grandfather's rice fields, but he still worked with the seed as a threshing operator in a chaffing mill. He'd married a woman from deep down in the bayou, but he still spent an hour every night scrubbing the day's work off his skin.

After my father walked out of the bathroom, I'd sneak in to flip over the soap he used in my hands, to find the place where the grime wore down the edges of the bar and his nails carved crooked lines, as if he was scratching at something deeper than dirt. There weren't many traces of my father in our home. Whatever he touched, I wanted to touch. Whatever he held, I wanted to hold. If he couldn't lift me up anymore, I'd lift up everything that passed under his hand. Maybe the bar of soap would turn into gold. Maybe it would transform me too, make me the boy Mama wanted: porcelain clean and chrome bright.

Usually while Papa scrubbed-up, he closed the bathroom door and entered a limbo world. I'd wait beside the door, listening to every movement, until he stepped out with a gleaming set of arms and legs, a scrubbed-up walking mannequin of a husband. The arms were no longer for me, though, and his twisted grin passed over my head like a dying comet. It was my mother he wanted.

But one day he left a crack in the door, just wide enough for a pair of spying eyes. His voice shouted at something in the room, then a buzzing and humming sound filled my head. Odd words shook my ears.

"*Bec mon* fucking *chou*!"

"*Vas tu faire* in your ass!"

The words were a foul smear of French and English, but in Papa's baritone voice, they sounded almost holy. He half-shouted, half-muttered with a rhythm that made him sound like a Catholic priest chanting the Hail Mary while chugging a bottle of the blood of Christ.

Holding my breath, I pushed in closer until I could see Papa digging his nails into the soap and splashing water all over the embroidered towels. I knew how hard it was to get clean. Every night, Mama ran her finger in my ears, down my neck, and across the back of my knees, checking for a missed spot, a smudge of dirt, or a line of sweat. Any sign of grime sent her eyes spinning and her hands waving. She'd testify to the lamp, the couch, and the ceiling about her unclean son. How hard she worked to bring me closer to the Lord, how fast I fell back into the mud. Again, she sent me back to bathe, two, three, four times a night until her finger ran smooth against my skin and her tongue clicked in approval.

In that bathroom, I figured Papa was working for her blessing too. I watched as he scrubbed his hands and arms with the bar of soap, then stripped off his shirt and rubbed his skin with a sponge. But when he dropped his pants, then his underwear, I moved back out of the light. The broad mass of his body cast a shadow, as if there were two men in the room, and the weight hanging between his legs hung like heavy figs. The sight of him startled me, and I didn't want to look or move any closer.

Until his voice rose again, and I pressed my face around the corner. That's when I saw my father, legs spread apart, leaning over the toilet. He looked thoughtful, concentrating hard on the problem in his hands. And in the quiet of his concentration, a song broke out of his mouth. Not a church song, but something in French, something that got his toe tapping the floor, something that sounded light and dirty.

"*Allons danser Colinda, bou-doum, bou-doum,*" he sang, "*bou-doum, bou-doum, Colinda danser.*"

Suddenly, Papa was singing a Creole song and laughing to himself. His back relaxed and his body rocked back and forth. He had no microphone, no backing band, but he was making music anyway. Not on the radio, not for a hall full of dancers, not even for my mother. So I pretended it was for me.

Soon, I started humming the song too, soft at first then louder and louder. "*Bou-∂oum, ,*" I repeated like a spell until a hand hushed my mouth. The words still echoed in my head, though, as my whole body lifted into the air. Above me, the ceiling sparkled like glitter and the brass globe spun like a wheel, its bright bulb throwing odd figures around the walls. The bathroom looked like a radiant sacristy, the sink a piscine, the drain a sacrarium. My hands flapped like a bird to touch the circle of shadows overhead. On my back I imagined a set of enormous wings. I floated and danced and sang in a whirling trance. Then I felt the grip of a pair of hands, and I looked down to see my father's face beaming. His light filled the room and all the objects glowed and our mouths moved in unison, singing the same song, round and round, until his grip slipped, his knees buckled, and my head hit the floor.

Right away, a welt rose on my crown, but I didn't cry. Even so, Papa's face turned ash-white, one eye twitched, and his hands drew back. He repeated a couple of words, over and over.

"There, there," he half-whispered, "now, now."

Then he stood and walked out the room with measured steps toward the calling voice of his wife. The sound of his steps echoed then died. For once, I didn't follow. I waited. Nothing much had happened — my father had dropped me, I had fallen — and yet the whole world had changed. A long time had passed since he picked me up. A long time would pass again. How much more must I wait? How far until there, there, Papa, and how long until now, now?

3.

MASKED BOY

For a long time, I crept around the house like a small ghost. I faded into the patterns of wallpaper when sliding down the hall, slipped through the keyholes of doors when leaving a room, crawled into the pages of books when escaping danger. And when Mama called my name, I kept my voice low and lips tight, talking not from my mouth but from the cavern of my seven-year old chest.

If I talked without a lisp, maybe she'd hear the boy she wanted, the one with a steady tongue. If I walked without a flap of my hands, maybe she'd see that solid boy, the one with steady feet and a steady future. Maybe she'd drop the whip then wrap her arms around me like pelican wings.

The boy Mama wanted had skin whiter than mine, skin that never reddened, never darkened. He hit balls with one crack of his bat, caught balls with one snap of his glove. On the mantel, his trophies glinted and glowed. That boy didn't hide in books; he leapt off the pages. He didn't slip through keyholes; he burst through the door. He squared off against danger, defended his name, and lifted his mother right out of the boggy swampland of Louisiana into some other state. That boy climbed roofs and trees, sailed through the air on ropes and wires, conquered roads and ditches with his mighty motocross bike. He turned shaggy fields of rice into shining forests of gold. He appeared in my window at night, with the moon buzzing around his head, yet lived down the street, under someone else's roof and someone else's name. Soon he'd loom over me, older, taller, stronger, with eyes unmasked, mouth unhinged, and body uncloaked.

When he entered the front door after work, my father stepped lightly, as if intruding upon another man's house. He knocked first then turned the knob slowly, unsure what scene he might confront. His son kneeling on hard tiles in the kitchen, with his hands threaded and head bowed. His wife pacing the floor, with white knuckles and a white-hot whip. The air cracking like dry straw. He unbuttoned his collar, unloosed his tie, and unhooked his belt. At the rice mill, he'd moved from machine operator to paper pusher, but he had no power here. Even when the scene shifted, with his wife whipping up meringue for a pie and his son sitting with his nose in a book, he spoke as little as possible, said almost nothing. Any word might light a match, might start a fire he couldn't extinguish.

At dusk I went in search of Papa outside, the only place Mama let him drink beer or play tunes. Long ago, he'd surrendered dominion over the fridge and the stereo. He commanded only a plastic ice chest and a plastic transistor from the tailgate of his pickup truck. He couldn't choke back a bottle of beer in his own living room, but he unloaded a six-shooter in the garage. He couldn't drop the needle on Bois Sec or Boozoo on the record player, but he cranked up zydeco and Cajun, dancehall and swamp pop, fais do-do and la la on the radio outside. In his garage of solitude, Papa sawed his legs across the concrete floor or sawed his hand across an invisible fiddle. As I watched, he conducted a frenzied Cajun band, lifted a frantic wife to her feet, lifted a fragile son to his shoulders, all while humming to himself.

When the song in his head stopped, he stared at his empty hands then lifted another half-frozen beer to his lips. No one knew the bullet in his chest, the vulnerability of his X-ray eyes to a weepy waltz about lost time. No one knew the storm in his ear, the supersonic echo of his wife's every want, every unmet need. No one knew the supernova under his crown, the magnitude of his strength, as he raised a graveyard of memories before his peeping son. All the Cajun men who'd ridden horses, ridden tractors, who'd raised houses, raised hell floated out the garage, over the yard. All his haunted heroes made no sound and never touched ground, yet they danced in a haze of air.

Some secrets held such power they had to remain hidden, not in a closet or at the bottom of a chest, but out in the open, where no one would notice.

Inside the house, Mama danced with no ghosts and entertained no gloom. She'd shelved the legends of her barefoot bayou childhood next to expired encyclopediae and outdated yearbooks. Instead, she read glossy magazines with manicured lawns and lives. Elsewhere, people breathed air without fumes, walked on land without ooze. Men made fortunes with ease, and women had maids and cooks and walk-in closets. Alone with her son, she romanced those men, conjured tales of another life, another husband, as she read each article aloud like a story. In a profile of quick fame or easy riches, she replaced another woman's name with her own. She punctuated each tale with the hyphen of her mouth and the bracket of her shoulders, determined to write a new ending. Yet Papa disrupted the fairy tale, disappointed her every day, dropping not a shiny briefcase by the door but a pair of dusty boots, not a stack of century notes but a few sawbucks, not a blank check but an empty grunt. He disappointed himself too, it seemed, as he sighed with the news of other men's triumphs. Over dinner, Mama spooned it out, night after night.

"That new couple at the end of the block just booked a cruise. On a *ship*."

"The insurance broker and his wife toured New York City and saw show after show. On *Broadway*."

"The psychiatrist next door took his wife to brunch. *Jazz* brunch. At a *hotel.*"

His own paycheck barely covered the mortgage and Mama's endless renovations. While Papa conducted an orchestra of memory in the garage, Mama directed a theater of fantasy in the house. She raised fairy tales on the walls with elaborate murals and flocked velvet featuring European villas or abstract bursts of arabesque. She suspended fables from the ceiling with octopus-armed chandeliers, set to glow with dancing flames. She arranged and rearranged a royal court of furniture with French Provincial, Spanish Colonial, then Hollywood Regency. She grouped chairs into Conversation Corners, grouped figurines into Curiosity Cabinets, and grouped landscapes into Gallery Clusters. The plush carpet whispered of richer times ahead. The glass sliding door gazed back at her in wonder, along with her creeping son.

Long ago, her own mother was confined to a cinder-block house in the projects, and her grandmother dwelled under a tin roof with mud and moss stuffed into cracks for insulation. She missed not one iota of the past, not one half of her half-breed legacy. There were no graveyards in her view, only future fields to travel. She missed not one minute of lost time. Her watch only wound forward, and her calendar only marked the next day. Tomorrow rose up in spires and stairways, in white peaks and gold palaces. Even if no one visited, she dusted, scrubbed, bleached, polished, and shone every dark surface of the house.

Then she covered every dark inch of her face with pale cream and frosted powder, and she crowned her dark hair with a sparkling cloud of spray. She was no one's ash-girl, no one's swamp woman, and she refused to stand still on sinking land.

Of all the men she secretly romanced, one stood taller, blonder and broader than the rest, with a wingspan that reached over half the block. The man who lived next door: the psychiatrist. He had diplomas—plural—on his office wall. He had *The New York Times* and *Wall Street Journal* delivered to his front door. He had two cars in the garage, one for his diamond-faced wife. He had broker statements and stock reports in his mailbox. Yes, she looked. And a son so grown up that he slept on his own, in a camper in the driveway. Thirteen, he collected ribbons, medals, and trophies not in art or drama or reading rallies but in real races and real games played at night under the stars and a bank of stadium lights. In high school, she'd watched a boy just like him bat his way into the minor leagues before she dropped out to marry my father, all because he had a car and a job in another town.

"I could've been the wife of a Yankees pitcher," she announced in an exaggerated whisper. "Or a heart surgeon. I could've had a car of my own and a credit card and a house decorator and a whole living room of ladies over for tea. Who knows? I could've married a psychiatrist."

Her voice trailed off as she stared me down.

"You," she said. "You can go over there, meet the boy. Make friends. Who knows? Anything can happen."

Mama looked over my head—and past my age and height—to see me catching balls in the backyard for the neighbor's son, the *psychiatrist's* son. Maybe he'd teach me how to stop prancing on tiptoes and flapping hands in the air. Maybe he'd teach me how to catch a ball, hit a ball, score a point. How to be the boy she wanted.

Out of a haze one sweltering day, the neighbor's golden boy passed right by me, inches away, jack-hammering his bike. His legs pumped straight up and down but his body piked forward at an odd angle, as if he was going to leap from the handlebars into an imaginary pool of water. He'd passed me on that bike nearly every afternoon but never looked twice. He never looked long at anyone though. Down the block, everyone called him Flash, with his blond hair and legs like lightning. At high school, he ran track and ran from diamond to diamond on the baseball field and from post to post in the football stadium. There was no sport, no game he couldn't win. Before me now, he pedaled right into a gray cloud shooting from the tail pipe of a truck crawling along our street. Once a week, that truck sprayed a fog of insecticide over the lawns and ditches and sidewalks and over the houses like a sprawling but invisible mosquito net. At the first sign of the truck, all the mothers shut doors and windows. Yet the boys mounted bikes, crashing in gray clouds and falling onto hot asphalt, dizzy with fumes and speed. With a chance to disappear too, I hopped on my bike and followed Flash as close as I could while he pedaled circles and circles around the truck until our tires collided, and we both fell into a ditch. When I stood up, half as tall and half as old, he eyed me suspiciously, as if unsure who I might be, then grinned and nodded toward his camper.

"Let me see it," he said, soon as I stepped inside.

When I looked down, I saw a trail of blood on my leg and a tear in my shorts. Flash dropped to his knees to examine the wound but soon started rubbing spit on his hand and rubbing his hand on my thigh until it turned red. His mouth broke into a radiant smile, and a shadow-line shone over his lip. His breath stopped, his eyes widened, and I half expected him to burst out of his shirt with a chest of armor and a clap of thunder. Instead, his look softened before darkening with a click of the bulb swinging overhead. I couldn't make out his face or the outline of his body. The room blurred into a purplish black, and my ears echoed with the sound of shuffling feet.

"Boo!" Flash shouted behind me then exploded in laughter as light shone from the ceiling again. "You like games?" he asked.

I nodded, not sure what he meant, as he pressed a pack of chewing gum in my palm and a bandage on my knee.

In the following weeks, Flash picked up not a single bat with me in the backyard and tossed not one ball my way, yet he ordered me out of clothes and into a bed sheet for a Greek council in his father's office. A knot held the sheet on one of my shoulders, like a toga, while he stood with a paper crown on his head and issued accusations and declamations with a wave of the hand. Back in the camper, he dressed me in one of his old Halloween costumes, a magic elf, while we played a game he called a "campaign" with lots of monsters and wizards. The rules confused me, yet I knew it was all make-believe. I'd watched Papa perform a dance with ghosts in the garage and Mama practice serving tea to invisible ladies in the living room. So when Flash threw a hood over his head or spoke through a cone, I did what he said and did my best to pretend. He'd hang a tarp in the window with holes punctured to make pinpoints of light, like twinkling stars. He'd flip the card table over so that it was a power station with interplanetary antennas, or he'd throw a blanket across the top for a Batcave. On the walls, blacklight posters glowed with a confusion of swirling galaxies, safari animals, and smiling aliens. In one, Spiderman shot a lethal web at some unseen villain, while his red mask shimmered and his arms bulged.

Sometimes, Flash acted out scenes from the posters. He talked and talked and made up stories and new games, and I took it all in, waiting for my part. At the end of each game, he made a big show of giving me what he called my "payoff." Chewing gum in cartoon wrappers with glow-in-the-dark colors. Trading cards with grotesque villains, some just boys, caught up in an endless series of doom: rising from a city sewer with a red face and a nuclear fist, standing before a busted window and a moon bubbling like tar, or sitting butt-naked on a crack in the earth with a mushroom cloud overhead. Bloody knives, spaghetti limbs, crossed paths, and twisted necks. These were bad guys, I knew, but the cards smelled like bubble gum and candy hearts. I liked their red faces, their atomic hair, and I liked that the golden boy liked them, too.

"A pack of weirdos," he called them but spread the cards on the table and told a different story for each in a near whisper, as if we were best friends talking in the back of class or sharing a secret in the middle of the playground. He pulled me closer and closer to him in the camper and even promised to open the chest he kept locked near the bed. Yet he never talked about school and never showed me his track medals or anything that didn't come from a game box. And he never once challenged me to a bike race or called me over when other boys filled his backyard.

One day, though, with the shades drawn and the door latched, he unlocked and opened that chest. Inside rose a tall stack of fairy tales and an even taller stack of comic books, with the names of superheroes and supervillains emblazoned on the covers. He already was magic to me, Flash, and he seemed to live in more than one realm. A star pupil at school, a popular jock on the block, a game master in the camper. And since he started calling me over, Mama's hand whipped meringue and sweet batter more often than she whipped me. The counter filled with ribbon-laced pies and medallion-shaped pralines. I ate them in silence, not wanting to break the spell. I was not her golden boy, not yet, but I was getting close. Whatever magic Flash had stored inside his chest, I wanted.

While I gazed at the stacks and stacks of books, I heard a click. Then the room went purplish-black again. I waited for Flash to yank on the light and pop up behind me. But instead I heard clothes falling to the ground, first the thud of shoes then the snap of a belt and the hiss of a pair of pants. The room got darker and there was no sound at all. Until I heard a voice in my ear, gruff now and suddenly older.

"Boy," Flash said, as he led my hand to his leg. "Put your mouth here."

Then he clicked on the light. His eyes were hidden, blocked by an oversized pair of sunglasses. His shoulders were wrapped by a man's blue velvet robe with a wide shawl and someone's monogrammed initials over the heart. He looked like a comic book character, straw-gold hair, egg-white skin, and a shape that ran into a V. Yet he was naked under the robe, I knew, and I could feel the 3-D burn of his stare, could smell his scent too, the barely sweet musk and the slight char. My head filled with an odd vapor, and my skin seemed to peel away. What did he want to do now? When would it start? How long before he threw off the giant robe he wore like a cape?

"Here's the deal," he said, pulling on the sash. "Suck it and take your pick. Suck it and take any book you like."

Right then, the floor turned to hot glue.

Flash kept those sunglasses over his eyes, but I could tell he was staring me down, waiting for my answer. Yet I couldn't say a word any more than I could move a foot. I froze, dumbstruck by the figure of the neighbor's son, looming larger and larger before me, as large as a full-grown man. His chest inflated with air, and his shoulders widened until his whole frame seemed to double in size. His legs towered over the comic books, and his hands stretched toward the walls on either side.

Next, the giant Flash dragged out a hurricane fan, a big whirling machine, and turned the blades on high. With the rushing air, his robe began to billow, and he looked like a superhero facing a menace or a wizard fighting back a monster. Before my eyes, he spread his arms like wings and pulled me close.

"Suck," he said.

As my mouth opened, my tongue stiffened and I started to choke, but his hand clutched the back of my neck. Then, in a softer voice that brushed against my ear, I heard him say it, say the word that split me forever.

"Fuck," he said.

Finally I opened my mouth to say, "Yes."

In an instant, his hand turned into a muzzle, his face swelled into a balloon, and he pushed me back on the twin mattress, pulled my pants down to the floor. My shoes kept kicking against the pullout bed, but I kept my mind on the payoff. Soon he would stop and hand me another trading card, another pack of gum and a comic book too. But as his body kept rubbing against mine, instead of bubblegum or candy hearts, an awful smell rose around him, sharp as bleach, and my skin began to burn. His hands whipped my back and sides, so I closed my eyes. With a huff of breath, I tore in two. Half of me pushed my face deeper into the pillow and wanted him to do it again, to beat and break my skin, and half ached and ached and only wanted him to stop.

"Don't tell anyone," Flash warned me after. "Don't say anything."

Although he was thirteen and I was seven, I knew what he did was wrong, what I did was wrong. The burnt-match scent of danger filled the camper. His hair was wet with sweat, nearly black now. An alarm of words rang in my ear, and a flare of red shone in his eyes as he slapped a single comic book in my hand.

"Payoff," he said.

One time. That was it. Once was enough, though, to take me away from Mama and Papa for good, to lift me too high and drop me too fast, to teach me too soon the lesson Mama had wanted me to learn: how to be a solid boy.

"Don't tell anyone," he said again.

But I didn't answer. Instead, I dug my arms into the open chest and lifted a towering stack of books. I hugged the books close and kept my lips shut. Even so, my body stretched inside its skin, and my face pushed against its mask. At home, I might still flinch when Mama raised the whip across my back. Yet I wouldn't slip through a keyhole. I wouldn't creep like a ghost. I'd square off against danger. I'd learn the power of my legs and learn to run faster than Flash, faster than lightning. I'd race out of the boggy swampland alone. I'd open my mouth to the sky, and sooner or later, I would tell.

For now, here I am, Mama, the boy you always wanted: your fabled son, rising with the moon in the window, with a new set of cards in hand and a disc of gold spinning overhead. Here I am, Papa, your little dark hero, running in a cape, running on winged feet, dancing in the lost air. See me run. See me spin. See me tear myself in two. Guess it now, guess my new name?

4.

ALTAR BOY

If there'd been no greased animal, the Courir would've been no more than an unholy run in the mud. In the bayou parishes, Mardi Gras called not for a run but a chase, with unmarried men fifteen and over snapping burlap whips in the air and onto the backs of other men in their path. Once flogged, the young men sank to their knees in ritual prayer while a ragged pelt was laid on their shoulders. Then they sprang back to their feet to chase a wet chicken, rope an oiled pig, or beg for pennies and pistolettes from the bystanders. The stingy were punished by revelers with willow branch whips on the rear and goat bladder bomps on the head. The revelers took turns riffling through the mean pockets, seizing dollar bills and loose change as loot while everyone else cheered the thievery as if the coins were raining from above, with beads and charms for all. At a manic high point, the unmarried men linked arms for a dance that had them moving almost can-can style with feet in the air, singing about a frog with a long tail and a fire underfoot. Finally the whole *fête* crashed with the butchering of a pig and the crowning of a queen, complete with a handmaiden dressed like a fairy.

Unlike the parades and floats in the city, the bayou krewes knew no king—and no law. The whippings might turn brutal, the theft might turn to rout, and the goat bladders might burst with beer. Their costume colors ran louder than any in the Vieux Carré, a riot of purple, green, and gold, along with stop-sign red or fireball orange, patched together with the rags of a pauper but in the fashion of a priest's cassock or a judge's robe. There was a *capitaine*, yes, but he was elected from among the drunkest. The honorary title went to the one who sucked at the beer bladder longest without pausing for breath. And when the run was done, they dunked him in a trough of ice water, stripped him of his *capuchon*, then dragged him to the steps of the church to await Our Lady of Prompt Succor and the mercy of the newly crowned queen, who offered him not the bounty of her lips but the bite of a cracklin'.

Of course, the next day everyone filed into that church with a fire in their belly and ash on their foreheads, as if all the revelry had only been conducted in the name of redemption. Yet at nine, I got the impression that it went the opposite way and that the day could last all year. Mardi Gras meant go in any direction, run anyway you wish. Between hunter or handmaiden, I already knew my direction. Between *capitaine* or queen, I already knew my wish. And by the end of Mardi Gras day, I meant to show my wings.

Those wings had sprouted early enough to bend my direction. After third grade, I was sent to a boy's camp in Ascension Parish, on the far side of Acadiana. Sacred Heart Academy reformed boys who didn't fit as scouts, as Cubs, Eagles, or Wolves. Boys who didn't fit at school, who didn't even fit their own skin.

"*Bien dans sa peau,*" Cajuns said about a man with a steady gait. They had other words for a boy uneasy on his feet. "Jenny Woman," some said under their breath. And no one bet on a boy with that name.

At the camp, no bets were on me, as I spent more time in the counselor's office than collecting badges in the field. Back at school, I'd been found "lurking" in the gym shower and "stashing" postcards of movie star hunks in my locker. The year before, I'd sent a carnation to another boy in class along with a cut-out heart. And long before kindergarten, I'd spoken with a girl's tongue and walked with a girl's hips. Mama ordered a doctor to insert a corrective wedge in my shoes, and Papa ordered the gym coach to "knock the lily off my stem." He punched me into every sport and every game only to see me land on my back every time, wood floor or grass turf. Just a month before the camp, a conversion specialist pronounced me cured after memorizing ball game scores and the long batting history of the only Cajun ever to pitch for the Yankees. But any kid at school knew there wasn't a test I couldn't ace or a game I couldn't flub. And my own pitching arm still swung like a girl tossing a bouquet from the altar.

My bent direction caused enough trouble by day that Papa could hardly look at me at night. He could raise the roof with a line of curse words and the back of a car with one hand, but he couldn't raise my hand to catch a ball aimed right at my nose or tackle a teammate half my size. He flinched at the sight of his son's swishy walk and fluttering hands on the field, he cringed at the sound of his son's stagey voice and show-tune lisp, so he disappeared at night to fix what he could in the workshop of his garage.

Mama, on the other hand, couldn't stop looking at me, as if she stared hard enough she might see the horns she'd missed at birth. My Bible-quoting mother could open the sky with a line of Holy Scripture. She could turn floor tiles to hot coals until you confessed every sin in your head, even the ones you'd yet to commit. She could fire hallelujahs through a cypress door. She could see through the walls of every room in the house, but she couldn't spank, slap, shake, or strike a satisfying answer out of me. Try all she might, Mama couldn't right my direction.

Her inquest charged the air:

Why was I singing to a naked G.I. Joe doll in my room?

Why was I—Sweet Jesus—sitting naked in the tub at midnight?

Why was I flapping my hands in my sleep like a bird?

Why was I walking from room to room in the witching hour talking to the air like an old woman in the attic?

Why was I waltzing around the house with a broom in my hand after all decent God-fearing people were asleep? Holy Mother of God, did I think I was a maid in a fairy tale? Was that it? Was she raising a fairy of a son?

When my voice sunk to my feet, she answered her own questions with the hot fire of her gospel tongue and the heavy rain of her hand on my back. I couldn't speak and couldn't answer, but I could see what she saw. Under the clouds of the Old Testament, my halo had tilted. Under the dome of our little town, my robe had parted.

Walking through the carnival streets, I quickly learned that Mama wore her own wings and shone her own colors. Her green eyes, a deep moss at home, lightened to a near gold. The flecks shimmered in the kaleidoscope of sun and foil and neon and revolving faces. Her raven hair shone with ombre against the flashing signs for spun-sugar candy. And her face glimmered and glowed without the red moth that she fought to cover in the morning mirror. Rather than burn her cheeks, the rays from all directions calmed her skin into a cool tint, almost the color of her palms. The globes of caramel apples brightened when she passed, and the round eyes and broad faces of men brightened too. Their noses flared and chins lengthened, drawing their heads into her light. Her slim satin mask seemed to reveal more than it concealed, as a rush of excitement darkened her lips and parted them again and again in a soft little gasp. She was the center of the world, this woman, and I wanted the face she wore.

On good days, Mama allowed me to watch as she made up her face with a foundation of thick white cream. Under that cream, the dark surface of her skin disappeared. The chicory color of her face troubled her, she confessed before the bright lights of her salon mirror. The copper red of her bayou Indian father crashed with the olive yellow of her French Cajun mother to make a wild color that Mama found hard to tame. Flashes of red would break out under the surface of her cheeks, or traces of the brooding Sabine would linger around the corners of her eye. She pouted and pulled at her skin, slapping the trouble spots then running a cooler hand over them until her face finally blanched into the lighter shade of the women in the fashion magazines—and in the front rows of the Catholic church. When her face paled, she seemed at once horrified and pleased, as if staring into a package filled with her childhood wishes but addressed to some other person.

She plucked at wild hairs that ran between her eyes with the pliers of her nails and rubbed at the wider edges of her lips until they drew into a thinner, neater line. Along the way, she dropped warning flags, little white tissues marked with her lipstick and flesh-colored sponges, damp from the fountain of her eyes. Like an altar boy, I swooped down to scoop up each tissue and pressed my lips on the red marks. She tossed her head back and laughed.

"Look at mama's boy," she said. "Can't get enough of my kisses."

But her kisses weren't the only ones I wanted.

On Mardi Gras day, all the men's painted faces seemed as fantastic as my mother's, twisted with all the gaudy colors of popsicles and all the greasy sheen of blood sausage. At first, those faces didn't frighten me. They thrilled me into laughter, and I felt the urge to point. There was a wide-mouthed pelican, with a plastic beak and tatty feathers. There was a long-nosed alligator, with a row of felt triangles on his back. And over there was a sharp-toothed wolf with dungaree shorts and moss-covered arms. I wanted to touch each one, to sniff the gamey musk of monster after monster, but their hands passed over me to reach for my mother, as they sniffed the taboo rose of her scent.

In the mass of men, then, I could disappear, so I left my mother's side for a tour of the booths and a concert of barkers. All around me, I heard the dying sounds of Cajun men, the horse-throated grunts and pony-high whines of their talking songs.

When a cup of gumbo hit a man's mouth, he whinnied with gratification, as if an invisible hand had just run down the slope of his neck. When he picked up a hot link of boudin, he whistled in anticipation as if to say this would be the one, the link that would take him back to the days of the Acadian cabin, rising high on cypress piers with bousillage in the walls and a

fraternity of boys in the attic. When he picked up a ruby slice
of watermelon, he wet his lips like a wolf as if to say no amount
of drink could quench his thirst, not even the bloody flesh of a
melon. Still, he wouldn't stop trying. He'd chug back cup after
cup of beer, bourbon, and any backwater hooch for a souvenir
taste of the man he used to be.

Every Cajun man was, in some real way, smaller than the
man before him. From across the parade path, I could see my
own father shrink behind my mother as the carnival men danced
in the street and the tent barkers ate and drank with fiery eyes.
For a while, I watched him watch her until her face was eclipsed
by one of the young revelers. My father sank into his judge's
robe when it looked as if the teenager was kissing Mama. What
could he fix? He turned toward home. Then I turned my face
back to the parade.

Tall Capuchin monks and medieval friars passed by on
rickety hand-made floats, with twisting tassels and sequined
robes in tatters. Short comic book nuns stood behind them
in beaded wimples and garter belts, with balloon breasts and
flaming red wigs. They passed the steeple of the Catholic church,
the arch of the cattle feed store, and the altar of the recording
studio where Cajun bands sawed out the uneasy beat of a waltz.
They passed the bronze statue of the crooked governor whose
eyes seemed to follow you no matter what direction you moved,
as empty as a pair of pennies.

Like that governor, the eyes of every man wandered blankly. Like him, everyone wore a mask. Everyone flashed the nervous smile of a freed suspect. On this one day, in this one festival, everyone was someone else. The monks were camouflaged farmers, and the nuns, it turned out, were just boys in costume. Everyone could laugh at what they were not. Everyone could gawk at the made-up faces. But no one, not one Mardi Gras reveler in the whole town, looked straight ahead at the fact that they were dancing on a mass grave, marching a parade right over the dead ground of a phantom people.

In the Catholic church, death calls for last rites and a host of ministrations, but at Mardi Gras even the altar boy was drunk and the priest was absent without leave. So everyone kept dancing and the fiddles kept sawing the air, muffling the laughter of the two teenagers as they hog-tied my arms and slid lard over my body. One of them kept chugging back a bladder of beer while another dragged his foot into the dirt, like a pony gaming for a race. They'd spotted me in a booth trying on a plastic tiara.

"Little queen," they shouted in unison. "Little fairy."

Both were from Ascension, from Sacred Heart. Two of the older boys at the camp—young men, the priests called them— they'd been expelled from the same high school and had formed their own scouts: the Wild Boars. For Mardi Gras, they wore the choir dress of altar boys, each with a black cassock and a red sash, but at Redeemer they wore football jerseys and lace-up pants even off the field. They grunted in the halls, and chased sissy boys like me into corners and stalls. When they tugged at their laced crotch, I should've turned my head, but my eyes roamed again and again and my wishes rose up like flames. I wished for the touch of another boy, it's true, even at nine and even at camp. And the Wild Boars delivered that wish every time they cornered me. Once that summer, they chased me into a watery bog then yanked my wet trousers down to my ankles while I turned crawfish red.

On Mardi Gras day, though, they skipped the baptism and went straight for another sacrament. While my eyes flipped into my head, they delivered hard punches to my chest, hard jabs at my face, and stinging gobs of spit. The lard they smeared on me ran down my limbs in streaks, like greasy ribbons, as they started calling animal names in my ear. My legs began to buckle, and my lungs emptied out. Then the sky opened up and a black cloud of rain fell over us. I went tearing out of their carnival tent toward the streets of town. The grease seemed to speed me through the air as I pulled further and further away from the Wild Boars, but their grunts were echoed by others who spotted that tiara still on my head and a tassel of feathers trailing my feet. The grunts rose to shouts and roars and fiery words. Papa stood on the sidewalk behind Mama, his hands covering his face, while she lifted up her eyes and spirit fingers in prayer. Any other boy might've run in their direction, might've repented in a white-hot flash. But my legs wouldn't move that way, and my arms were still bound behind my back, so I ran past my parents, past the crowd of revelers in the street and right to the top of the marble steps of the church where I waited for my wings, waited for my *capitaine*, waited for the whole of carnival to end in ash.

Near midnight, I awoke on the steps with a tapping sound in my ear. It was a frog, a man-sized frog waving and tapping at me. When I looked again, I saw it was my father. He'd shed his robe for another costume, but the tail had been cut and one ear folded over, making him look more like a green bulldog than a frog. He said nothing to me, but I felt something move in my shoulders as he loosened the rope and set my wrists free. He said nothing, but he sang a Cajun song called "Saute Crapaud" which had just two lines.

"Jump, frog, your tail will burn;

But take heart, it will return!"

All the next day, the words echoed in my head until I found myself singing them too, not high and bright like a show tune but fast and furious like a Cajun two-step. My feet moved to the jig with a hobble on one leg and a lift on the other. Round and round and round and round until my head spun and the roof opened and a coin of light shone in the attic room like a small crown. I put a finger to the light then to my forehead. With the sound of my father's knock, it was time for the walk back to Prompt Succor, time for the Imposition of Ash.

5.

FLOUNDER

The place was so upside-down, so higgledy-piggledy that direction made no sense at all. When the crooked bayou shifted course and snaked back on itself, when upstream ran down and east bank sat west, then all compass lost meaning. Not even the three boys racing around the marsh could tell you which way they were headed. Their foxfire movements lit one side of the bayou then another, sending lines crashing into circles, shifting shapes in the air. Even so, they knew one direction for sure: the way to be a real boy. For nearly a week, I watched my cousins race each other for that end until I went dizzy and cross-eyed with want, until I finally turned upside down too.

By the time I reached eleven, Mama had tried everything to make me a real boy: the school counselor, summer camp, the silent treatment, speech therapy, a G.I. Joe doll, a NFL football, a military crew cut, a long belt across my back, and an endless streak of Holy Scripture. None of it, not one thing, had worked. In the classroom, I may have become the star pupil, but on the playground and the football field—where it really mattered—I remained twinkle toes, a Tinker Bell with light feet and butter fingers.

So on my birthday, Mama announced a new plan. She'd bring me to the bayou cove where she'd grown up, where she'd seen men and even teenage boys rise out of the water with forty-pound nets of shrimp, where she'd seen her own father wring the head off a chicken and tear the skin off a buck like he was removing wrapper from a candy.

"If any place can fix you," she said, "it's the bayou."

She didn't step out of the car or even stop the engine. Instead, she lowered the window, fingered a wad of bills from her purse, and pressed them into her sister's hand with a click of her tongue.

"Make him be," she said.

Then she declared, "You can't be a real boy, not until you learn how to handle a knife and run the sharp end over fresh kill."

The way she described it, learning to be a real boy was nothing more than learning a sport. But I knew there had to be some magic in it since none of the signs were clear. The more I tried to play along, the more I got the game wrong. The more I tried to stand straight, the more I looked bent.

If I expected a set of directions from my Pentecostal aunt, though, I was let down. She outlined no rules, issued no manual. After Mama left, she just folded the bills without a word then fished a yellow pill from her jean skirt and slipped it onto her tongue. As she swallowed, her throat moved like a lizard's calling out to another across the yard, but she didn't speak. The towering bun on her head quivered as she shrugged her shoulders and headed back to the paper-thin house.

They must've smelled the wincing garlic of the beans and the sweet butter of the yellow cornbread. Something brought the three boys out of the bayou and out of the woods. Running hard and fast, my cousins were spinning dirt devils, driving clouds of black dust into the air. They ran and ran, whooping like a pack of pretend Indians, and I suddenly wanted to slip into costume, to play a role of my own.

But the boys hardly noticed me as they pushed past each other to race for the supper table. They called out positions, first, second, third chair. I tried to imagine how they came by that order and by the stains on their shirts. Maybe Hog stole an egg from the neighbor's roost and swallowed it whole, eggshell, yolk, and all. Maybe Duck wrestled with an alligator, stuffing his mouth with marshmallows and pinning down his webbed feet with arrowheads. Maybe Coon sank his teeth into a chicken's neck, and that's why blood ran down his collar. I'd seen those things at carnivals, men chasing frantic chickens and greased pigs, seen blood spilled in the name of Mardi Gras and manhood, and heard stories about my own voodoo-practicing strongman papère, but I'd never seen boys up close after handling animals for sport. It put air in their chest and a sense of self in their face.

The biggest and oldest at thirteen, Hog, plunked down in the only chair with arms then hoisted himself up so that he ruled over the rest of the table.

"I got the captain's chair," he hollered, "I get the ham bone tonight!"

The other two boys groaned then fought over a pack of crackers and a liter of soda. Each one, it seemed, had to claim a prize before he could eat, and eating itself became a sport as the boys raced against time and each other for a cast-iron pot of red beans and rice.

Coon, the youngest, had crescent moons around his mouth and the barely handsome features of a midnight bandit. His fingers, though, were long and thin, as if they might be more comfortable on a piano than around a knife. He had a way of turning his seat into a rocking chair. Always in motion, always tilting back and forth. His eyes revealed flecks of green in the light. Of the three, his grin glowed the brightest, as if all that rocking was the product of an unseen electric current running right down his spine. That spine gave him a bearing his older brothers lacked and made him seem sharper. Already, I felt myself bend, felt my hands twitching under the table and my feet lifting off the floor. Already, I wanted to touch his skin, to feel his shock.

Before I could even touch my fork, a sudden commotion at the table broke out when Hog announced that he single-handedly hauled in—for a moment—a thirty-pound flounder then lost it to an evil undertow.

"You ain't never even seen a thirty-pound fish much less reeled one in," Coon snorted to set the record straight.

"I swear to God and piss on a cracker," Hog shot back, "I oughta know what the fish weighed. It was *my* hand on the rod."

"Your hand weren't nowhere but on your own damn rod," Coon said, and Duck let rip a laugh.

My aunt's bun nodded from side to side. I looked for a flash of anger or a sermon on dirty talk, but she just steered another spoonful of beans into her mouth while the boys erupted into a full-scale fight. Soon, Hog was on the floor pinned by his smallest brother, crying every filthy name until he hit the magic one: fag. Once he choked out that word, every utensil, every dish became a weapon, and the boys tore down the hall to their room where it sounded as if a hurricane were chewing up furniture and shredding the sheetrock.

At that point, my aunt walked over to the glow of the TV, switched on a program called *Hour of Power*, and seemed to be sleeping with her eyes open. With that magic word still ringing hard in my head, I stared at the glow from the couch. There was a lot of talk about Sodom and a battle to end all battles and the need to raise money. I fell asleep to a phone number and a set of directions flashing in yellow on the screen.

In the morning, the TV was still on and my aunt was still sitting up, with a minister's blonde wife shedding tears, but the boys were nowhere in sight. If the screen door hadn't been hanging open, I might've believed they jumped out the window or punched their way through the wall.

At first, I was relieved they were gone. I didn't want to find myself in the middle of a dish-flinging wall-shredding storm. And I didn't want to find myself at the end of that word: fag. But then I thought of Coon, his bright grin and the way he rocked back and forth in his chair, and I set out to find the boys. All around the house, I heard their whooping sounds rise and fall like battle cries, but they never came into view. Instead, their voices flew in animal bursts. Then the air quieted down to an eerie stillness, so still that I could hear the toads warning of rain. Overhead, the sky blackened a bit, and I felt sure that I'd never catch up with them, that I'd never be a real boy.

So I headed back into the house to see what I could find in my cousins' room. When I opened the door, I saw three single beds all in a row, but two of the mattresses hung off their frame, as if the boys had used them for slides or trampolines, and the rest of the room was a wreck. Pillow stuffing scattered across the floor, sheets rolled into lumpy balls, clothes spilled from drawers, and the entire closet coughed out its contents. Mismatched shoes, chewed-up belts, a deflated inner tube, and stacks of yellowing comics ran from the closet door into the room, as if someone had been digging for a treasure or a hidden way out. Rusted pots and pans, crusted over with a sulfurous powder, hairy ribbons of moss, and what looked like chicken's feet.

Then I spied it: a blunt-edged butcher knife in the back corner. What were my cousins doing with that knife in their closet? I imagined them playing butcher in the bedroom, holding the knife over the body of a deer, or lifting it overhead like a comic book hero about to plunge a blade into the heart of the enemy. I imagined them wielding the knife like a bayonet or a javelin, holding the sharp end to the neck of an opponent.

Next I caught sight of a broom and hit on a plan. I'd clean it all up, the whole mess. Then the boys would have to notice me. Maybe they'd even take me into the woods on their next run.

Quickly, I went to work cleaning the room and setting everything in place while the wobbly fan nodded from side to side. With twinkling feet and twitching fingers, I sorted shoes, hung pants, rolled-up belts. Like a bird twittering over an untidy nest, I stacked boxes, folded T-shirts, and shook out sheets. I swept every inch of the floor as if I wore wings, dipping the broom up and down. I tugged each mattress onto its frame and tried lying on top. None of them felt right, but I finally fell asleep on the bed nearest the door.

Then, with a great burst, the door flew open and all three boys fell into the room, already holding their sides from laughter.

"Look at the new maid," Hog said soon as he saw what I'd done.

"What are you doing?" Duck asked, "Playing house?"

Then Coon shut everyone up by shouting, "Fag."

For a moment, hearing that word didn't bring the roof down, didn't send plates flying, didn't even burn my own ears. Instead, the whole room came into focus: the first time I ran a finger over the chest of G.I. Joe, the first time I showered in the boys' locker room, the first time I ran my hands over a football jersey then ran out the door with the smell of boys in a cloud around my head. *All right*, I thought for a moment, *all right*. But then I remembered Mama, remembered that my cousins were still in the room. I thought I'd been invisible in their home. Now, I worried they could see straight through me. Now, the word they spoke out loud burned my ears, and it sounded as if Coon was calling out my secret middle name. He stared at me with a pair of shimmering eyes, daring me to disagree.

"Fag," the other boys chimed in, and I saw myself pulled into a battle I couldn't win, until my aunt hollered down the hall to announce lunch. "*Manges! Manges!*" she said, and the boys raced again for the captain's chair. This time, Coon landed first. He and the other boys rushed through the pot of mushy red beans and rice, then Coon turned his attention to me.

"What kind of ball you play?" he asked, as he ran his hands over the arms of the chair and rocked it back and forth. Even at eleven, he already sported a dark line of hair over his lip.

"Ball?" I asked. In class, I sprang up with the right answer every time, defining difficult words, pointing to the capitol of any state on the map, any country on the globe. But there, before my cousin, I was not sure of anything, not even a small word like *ball*.

"Yeah, ball," he repeated, louder. "As in play. Do-you-play?" But I understood the question was really an accusation. Since there was no kind of ball I could play, I told my cousin that I wrote for the school paper, an "op-ed," I called it, and soda gushed out of his nose, while the other two boys joined him, howling with laughter.

"So you don't play but you do *write*," he repeated. He didn't have many words, but he knew how to use them, bearing down hard on one, easing up on another. I had a trunk full of words but couldn't lift even one with the same force.

"Write," he said again, only now he made it understood as "*Right!*"

Hog and Duck answered in unison, "*Right!*" They began to sing it back and forth as they spilled out the front door and went cutting a path—without me—to the woods. Coon looked over his shoulder and, for a moment, I thought I saw a grin.

In the city, my straight A's might've given me some leverage, but out in the country, they did me as much good as a feather pillow in a boxing match. If I was going to run with my cousins, if was going to get close enough to touch Coon, then I'd have to do something the other boys might do. Inside the paper-thin house, the *Hour of Power* still called for help, and my aunt's face now looked like the minister's wife, with tears falling harum-scarum down her face. Sodom was still rising, and money was still needed for the battle, and the minister still called out a number and a set of directions. Yet instead of taking a seat next to my aunt, I walked to the bank of the bayou.

Before me, the oily bayou gurgled. My aunt's house was downstream from a refinery, and—from time to time—the residue floated up in a dark sheen. The air bore a sheen too, a kind of rainbow glow, but it was dulled by a tint of yellow. And everywhere, the smell of sulfur rose up, a rotten egg smell undercut by the briny scent of the dead fish that sometimes floated in the bayou. With cataracts on their eyes and fungus on their scales, those dead fish looked like a sign from Exodus.

But there were live fish in the bayou too, and there was a rod near the bank. With no better plan, I dropped the line in the water and waited out the afternoon.

Just before dusk, the rod started twitching and—just then—the boys turned the corner from the woods.

"Shit-damn" Coon said, "you caught a fish."

Then he hot-footed toward the bank as I struggled with the rod.

"It's a twenty-pounder, at least," Hog said.

But Coon disagreed. "Naw, idiot, that fish ain't no more than two pounds."

Then he rolled his eyes and snorted. Duck took up the middle and judged it a five-pounder, but none of them had even seen it yet. The only way to settle the dispute was to yank the fish out of the water and lay eyes on it, and — since my hand was on the rod — I was expected to do it. I grew shaky and started stammering but managed to shout out, "I got it!"

But I didn't have it. I faltered and froze with the rod barely in my clutch. I stood there shaking, when Coon stepped beside me and hollered, "Arc it!" He threw his hands out in a pantomime next to me and suddenly I could smell the hard tone of his musk. His arm brushed against mine and I could feel his rough skin and the heat of his breath. My hands still shook but I tugged higher and higher and in another instant had the fish out of the water and onto the ground. It trembled and flopped around for a bit, both eyes quivering on one side of its head.

"It's a flounder," Coon declared then repeated in case no one had heard. "It's a flounder, all right."

Hog rolled his eyes but remained silent. What could he say? You could argue about the weight of a fish or the color of its scales. But the name of a thing had a certain authority to it.

That night, my aunt fried up the flounder in an iron skillet with mustard and cornmeal batter and hot oil until it was crisp and golden brown at the edges. For once, she hummed while she cooked, as if having more than beans put music in her mouth.

The boys let me sit in the captain's chair while they took turns telling the story of how the fish looked as it flopped around on the ground. Duck insisted that it was blue-black and that its eyes were blinking. Coon threw his fork down on the table and said, "That fish weren't no more blue than my teeth. It was gray and, anyway, fish don't blink."

Hog jumped up from his chair and fell to the ground in imitation of the fish gasping for air, while batting his eyes like a would-be starlet. Coon's hand slid over Hog's face like a hook, then Coon dragged him under the table and gave him a good hard kick. "That's it!" Hog said, as he pulled Duck down to the ground with them, and all three boys wrestled with each other for control of the words in the air.

I sat still in the captain's chair while my aunt walked over to the kitchen sink. She fiddled with a bottle and filled a glass with water. She popped a pill in her mouth and let her head fall forward before throwing it back, while her bun slipped from its clip. Then Hog rolled out from under the table and stood over Coon. "Fag," he said, pointing down to his brother, "You fag!"

In a furious cloud, they raced each other for their room, which exploded again. I imagined everything that I'd set into place flying into the air and landing in a tangle on the floor and figured I'd spend another night sleeping on the couch and another day cleaning up after the boys.

But then a voice down the hall hollered out, "Captain!" It was Coon's voice calling. "Captain Fag!" And I found myself running to my name.

When I got to the room, the scene was worse than I'd imagined. Not only were the mattresses back off their frames, but the boys were out of their pants and in their underwear, as if they'd been in the middle of changing into pajamas and started wrestling instead. Coon wore a sheet around his neck like a cape. What's more, he had Hog on the floor with that butcher knife at his throat, Duck had Coon in a half-nelson grip, and no one seemed able to budge.

"You gotta say it," Coon stared at me.

"Say what?" I asked.

"Say 'fag,' say which one is the fag."

All around me, the room started humming. Not a church tune but something lower, almost growling. That butcher knife shone in my eyes, and the fan buzzed in my ear, and I could hear the sounds of the TV, the minister and his weeping wife, and the sounds of the bayou water churning outside. In that moment, Coon's dare sparked like foxfire in the air. Each of my cousins lined up across the room, and each took on his name with greater force. Hog's chest swelled and nostrils flared, Duck's feet shuffled and weight shifted, and Coon's fingers stretched and eyes blazed. My own eyes filled with dust, as I stood on my toes, ready to take flight—but where? I started to speak but stopped. How could I answer the dare? How could I call any of them a fag? A tremor ran up my leg and into a coil just below my waist, and my forehead started to throb.

"Say it," Coon repeated, "say who's the fag."

"Say it!" Hog and Duck chimed in, "Say it!"

Just then, a stream of warm piss ran down my leg and onto the floor.

"Jesus," Coon said, as he dropped the knife. "Jesus."

In the days after, the boys let me into their circle, but they looked at me strangely, as if at any moment I might break down and start crying. They tossed underhand balls to me and showed me how to catch. They snared a wild rabbit and showed me how to twist its neck and run a knife under its flesh. They taught me how to hold a rifle and hit a tin can off a fence. My cousins even went on calling each other fag, down the hall and out in the marsh, but they stopped saying the word in front of me. Soon, I started to miss the sound of it, the heat of their eyes when it left their tongue and the wild mess it always set into motion. So on the last night, I decided to say it out loud. When Coon grabbed the butcher knife, in the middle of one of their fights, I threw my own neck under his blade.

"Me," I said.

"Me what?" he asked.

"I'm the fag."

And, in a flash, he dropped his underwear before the boys.

"Touch it," he dared me.

Right then, I went dizzy and cross-eyed with want. I lifted my hand into the air. But before I could touch anything, Coon brandished the knife and exploded in laughter, and the other boys laughed wildly too. They began running helter-skelter in a circle in the room, and I ran along with them. Round and round we went, the three beds spinning before me, the three boys spinning too. Everything spinning in circles before my eyes.

Then the whole world turned upside-down as Coon brandished the knife again and, with a bright grin, slid the blunt edge into my skin and I fell back onto the floor. He stood over me and ran the butcher knife into the slit on my hand a second time and a third until a tear opened and blood ran out.

"Faggot," he said, laughter still shining in his eyes, that word burning before us.

The name flashed in yellow letters before me, and I studied it for a long time. While the boys watched, my shoulders spread wide, and my stance widened too. My chest filled with air. There were no tears on my face, not one, but there was a fine mist everywhere as I opened my mouth, stretched out my arms, and unbent my knees.

"*Right*," I said, with a straight-edged tongue, "Faggot."

This time, no one laughed.

Even the TV went silent. No one called out a number. No one spoke of a battle to win or a direction to follow. Now I'd never be a real boy. Never. Under the sharp edge of a blade, at the tip of a knife, in a line of blood and dirt, the whole story just ended.

6.

SKINWALKER

Hulking over the desk, his elbow jerked back and forth with the thick inky lines of his pen marks. My lines jittered on the page, thin and curvy. My letters fell against each other like a row of hastily dropped gowns. Yet from the seat behind, I watched his letters rise up in sharp edges. Each word he wrote belted its trousers and squared its shoulders with the hard stance you'd expect of a boy at Holy Cross.

Even so, Blaze looked like no one else in junior high. In the morning, all tight corners and abrupt angles. By noon, taller, broader, threatening to burst from his clothes. He had heavy brows, dark unflinching eyes, and — rumor had it — saw through doors and chests and right into the heart of any subject. He never raised a hand in class yet barked out the answer to any question. He never knocked on a door yet nosed his way into any room. Already, stubble shadowed his chin and neck, which stretched half a length over any other boy. With the nuns out of view and the sun a halo overhead, his feet left the ground and he rose straight into the air with his arms out in the shape of a cross. Then his feet met the ground again, and he swung a tail like a whip. The other boys tightened their lips and glowered, but my mouth opened in wonder.

Before Blaze walked onto campus, anyone odd sat in the back with a shut mouth, sat solo in the quad, sat in the bleachers with a pair of stone feet. At least that's where I sat, the class sissy, the school puss. Even the yellow-eyed priest called me by that name when I lisped during Catechism.

"For the love of God," he said, "shut your puss, Puss."

On cue, all the boys jeered and made loud cat noises. From history, whether on campus or in textbooks, I'd learned what happened to puss boys: we ended up with knuckles in our face, a knee in our groin. Or worse: in gutters, gallows, and garrotes. Maybe the story was old, but it felt new every time I swallowed blood, and by eighth grade, I badly wanted a new ending.

Now the odd new boy sat wherever he wanted and spoke whenever he wished. Before us, Blaze walked right out of his skin into shape after shape. If the nuns returned and spied his tail, he snorted at their habits and pulled his brow into an arch or turned his uniform blazer inside out and ran barefoot across the church altar. Once, he unzipped his pants in the school quad and sprayed a perfect circle of flame-yellow piss around the flagpole. The fragrance rose in vapors, and the grass singed to a sooty black. Yet Blaze soon was the star athlete, the A student, the polymath, and he argued his way out of every corner with his blade of a tongue. I had no such weapon, so I hid behind his biggest-in-the-class back and prayed for cover. When he moved his arm or his head, I moved in turn. When he coughed, I coughed in echo. Before me, his hair shone like ink, and his shoulders spread like wings.

Even on the bench next to the principal's office, his head was unbowed, his shoulders unhunched. A nun had nabbed him for an inked image on the back of his hand: the reproductive cycle of the paramecium. He called it a study guide; she called it a cheat sheet. There was no exam scheduled that day, and it wasn't the first time Blaze had drawn on his skin. Sometimes in class, he coated an entire side of his hand with correction fluid. Then he wrote words in Latin or drew glyphs over the white field. I studied his hand drawings, like blue tattoos, while the nun jabbed a stick of chalk at the board, underlining lessons in our science class. A cloud of dust surrounded her head when she reviewed outlaw sexual phenomena, what she called "nature's deviants." Mostly, these were creatures that ate their sexual partners or changed their sex at will or mounted their own sex.

Dragonflies, gypsy moths, clown fish, black widow spiders. As the nun—and the biology section—droned on week after week, Blaze's drawings grew larger, more elaborate. The nun warned of skin poisoning, accused him of distracting the class and disturbing her, yet that only made him square his shoulders and widen his grin.

On the Friday when she eyed the paramecium on his hand, drawn in the "deviant" act of self-fertilization, her chest rose nearly to her chin in anger. Her eyes narrowed and her wimple shook. Days earlier, she'd denounced the paramecium, along with the earthworm and the slug as "lowly hermaphrodites." She'd marked an X in the air with chalk, as if to censor an illicit image. Yet Blaze's drawing featured a paramecium splitting itself in two. With a hairy footprint shape, it hardly looked pornographic. From a crooked angle, though, the nucleus might've passed for a nipple on a weirdly shaped breast. The nun stared at the sketch a long while, her chest rising and falling, then she announced a closed-book quiz: on the reproductive cycle of the paramecium. When I raised my hand to object—we hadn't even finished the lesson yet—she called me an accessory to the crime and accused me of plotting with Blaze to cheat. Then with two X marks overhead, she ordered us both to the principal's office.

The story made no more sense to the layman principal than it did to us, yet he asked Blaze to repeat parts over and over again as if he were memorizing the lines. Each time, Blaze added an extra twist, his hands scissoring the air into new shapes, while I sat on my own hands and screwed my mouth shut. A hellish fate awaited us, I was sure, already falling into the role of doomed criminal and damned sinner. Extreme punishments flashed before me: tongue tearer, knee splitter, thumbscrew. No doubt, if my clothes were pulled away, I'd be revealed as a quivering hairless animal. Yet the principal hardly even looked in my direction, and Blaze faced the desk while a pair of antlers seemed to crown his forehead. He bucked against every charge made by the nun, not just the cheat sheet but accusations of disorderly conduct, destruction of school property, and defiance of the dress code. Blaze turned each charge into a joke, delivering the punch line with a jab of his hand. After examining the paramecium tattoo, the principal coughed, stood up and hitched his pants. From a drawer, he pulled out a long paddle that all the boys called the Ugly Sister. Passing in the hall, you could hear a boy let loose a muffled shout when that rough cypress hit his rear end. Most of the time, the principal executed the law of the church and the rules of the school with more force than any priest. Yet when Blaze stared across the desk and locked eyes with him, tapping the floor twice with a heavy foot, the principal brought the paddle down on the chair instead, air whistling through the holes. After several loud hard smacks, he laid it down and hitched his pants a second time. Sweat glistened on top his lips. His hands shook a bit and his eyes creased with near-laughter. Then he looked long and hard at Blaze.

"What kind of lizard?" he asked again.

"Whiptail," Blaze said. "The all-lady lizard."

"And what did the Sister call it?"

"Parthenogenesis."

"Right," the principal said, with a hand to his shaking mouth. "Virgin birth."

Whether Blaze had mesmerized the principal into releasing us, I couldn't be sure. Yet free of the paddle and free of school for the weekend, he turned his eyes and looked straight at me for the first time.

"Come over," he said. It wasn't a question, so I didn't answer.

Instead, as if surrounded by a narcotic cloud, I followed the skinwalker home, lights bursting in my head and sounds echoing in my ears. You could be odd and not get flogged—not even in the principal's office? You could speak up and not get strangled? You could stand up and not get kneecapped?

Shifting from cloven hooves to spotted paws to the long whirling feet of a sprinter, Blaze dashed through his house, throwing off the school uniform and picking up a bottle of cola and a bag of Roman taffy. In his backyard, he jumped onto a trampoline and shouted after me to join him. As soon as I climbed up, he leapt from his haunches, the canvas bounced me into the air, and he exploded in laughter. My ears, oversized and nearly pointed, flashed with heat and I could feel them turning red. My arms prickled with every little hair standing needle-sharp on end, like a set of quills, and my nose filled with the smell of grilled meat and ripe fruit and wet grass and damp earth. All around, the world rose up and down in a shaking blur while blood rushed from my hands to my feet and back again. Under it all, I smelled a strong musk that flared my nostrils and dizzied my head. I wanted to remain weightless, high from the trampoline, from the heat, from thoughts of Blaze, but one leg overshot the frame and I landed with a splat on the ground.

Through my shirt, you could see my spastic rib, the one that pulsed with a strange twitch anytime my chest filled with too much air. Blaze crouched over me and pulled up the tails of my shirt. His eyes widened at the sight. That rib looked blue now, and it quivered out of sync with my breathing, making my whole chest throb like an animal under a spear. Then he looked closer and found my birthmark, a crimson-colored arrow on one side of a nipple.

"Deviant," he said then repeated it louder. "Lowly deviant!"

He howled between laughs and spat a mouthful of cola on the ground. His eyes glared, daring me to disagree. He'd invited me over for just this reason, I guessed, so he could pin me with an exclamation mark.

For a moment, I stood still as the breath rushed in and out of my chest. Then I jumped back on the trampoline and jumped into the air with that word ringing in my ear. *Deviant*. The nun had said it in class, of course, too many times, but never in the way Blaze said it, like a grunt of recognition. The word rang inside my head in echo after echo. All the perfume of the world rose up again, along with Blaze's face, his unblinking eyes and jutting chin and his mouth open wide in easy laughter. Soon, I overshot the trampoline once more and landed on my back, breathless, wordless.

The skinwalker stood over me, no longer grinning. His face the face of a sphinx. He stopped breathing too, it seemed, and his eyes shut for a long moment. Would he open those eyes soon and see a coward, a puss? Would he see a suspect boy? Would he jeer and catcall me like all the others?

When his eyes opened again, Blaze shook his head, tugged his lips on the cola bottle, then spat a caramel waterfall over my face. The ground fell away, and my whole body rose up. Blaze locked eyes with mine. Weightless, I opened my mouth in the shape of an O, letting the cola and spit rain into my throat while his grin returned and widened. Under his steady eye, I grew out of my shoes and floated over the backyard. I floated out of my clothes too, driven into a daze with his mouth on my neck and his hand on my waist. Master of letters, master of shapes, he cast that kind of spell.

In his bedroom that night, I kept my face to the pillow. When I was sure that he'd fallen asleep, I opened my eyes and turned toward him. Blaze slept with his shirt and pants off, and the sight of him thrilled me. My ears burned and my throat was dry and I knew every why. Why the priest mocked me at Holy Cross. Why the boys taunted me. Why my letters were odd curlicues, feathers and fans, ribbons of silk. Next to the skinwalker, I wasn't a standup boy or even a daredevil. I was only an accessory to the plot, a stock character, an end page waiting to be filled.

Yet now, in his bed, I didn't care that I couldn't match Blaze, that my own letters failed or that I was the sissy, the puss. As I lay alongside him with the rustle of sheets, his heart beat in my ear. I bent my hand, slid it under his arm, and musk rose around me. Heat rose too, followed by a grunt deeper and longer than all words. I drew my fingers back and pressed them against my face. Then the bed filled with steam. Grinning wide, with his long teeth, the skinwalker rose over me and clawed into my skin, the blood glistening before running off in tears. A set of initials branded me, three letters in ink, a fresh tattoo on my arm. My brow pulled into an arch. Maybe I'd never turn into a boy like Blaze, maybe I'd never square my shoulders or sharpen my tongue, maybe I'd never walk out of my skin or master anything at all, but he was my author now, and I was his sentence.

7.

REVELATOR

Late at night, with a perfumed wrist and a sudden click of her tongue, Mama put the magazine in her lap aside to tell me cautionary tales—odd, twisting stories about her outlaw father, about how he punched his way from parish to parish in lower Louisiana in pursuit of a ring and a championship belt. After quitting the ministry, he sought fortune as a boxer then left the Bayou State for work as a croupier, a bookie, and finally a bounty hunter, but a rash broke out on his hands each time some Texas boss in pointed boots called him a coonass. Did those cowboys think he was an animal? A trash-eating animal in a mask? Other times they called him

Otterfoot. Did they think he was a web-toed weasel? He'd show them; he'd shift his shape again. Now he was a snaggle-toothed wolverine, a claw-footed bobcat. Now he was a fox-eared traiteur, a swan-necked revelator. And now, *now* he was the hot tongue of breath over their head and the hairy finger that tapped on the window at midnight before the panes exploded and the house burst into flame. He was a rebel-yelling prophet, a vein-hunting warrior, a junk-shooting preacher. And if he was an animal, he was a champion *loup-garou*, a teeth-gnashing, bone-crunching werewolf.

Until the day they finally wrestled him onto a gurney and into a hospital and shot voltage through the electrodes on his head. Once, when I was eleven, Mama brought me to meet him. He was living in a cinder-block government home with a woman who had the same odd name as him and two boys who took turns sitting on one knee. The other knee was gone, the fabric of the pant leg dangling like a lady's handkerchief. His hair ran onto his back in a tight double ponytail, making his nose look sharp and long. His teeth were sharp and long too, all yellow and twisted. Syringes lined his dresser like firearms. You could smell the riot of perfume. Soon, he'd be dead, not of old age, though, or disease or even an overdose. No, he couldn't live in one shape, and he couldn't bear that he'd been robbed of wild thought by strangers wearing surgical masks.

Before I reached high school, Mama told me other tales about her father and his people, the Sabines, impossibly poor half-breed shrimpers and swamp-dwellers who—legend had it—were swindled by a pack of strangers bearing gifts. Men with smooth suits and smooth hair walked onto their land but with a rough speech that confounded the Sabines. The strangers spoke with no tone, even when their words ran into knots. At their feet, the Sabines saw overfilled baskets of rich meats and rare fruits they couldn't grow or buy on their own. They knew the taboo of foreign food, knew the sin of greed. Their tables already were laden with thick gumbo, giant shrimp, and blood sausage. Yet with hungry eyes, they quickly took the baskets and signed a stack of contracts without ever looking straight at the faces of the strangers. After feasting off the food, they grinned with satisfaction and rubbed their stomachs. Then their grins widened, and their eyes widened too. Soon, a fever broke out. Whole groups of men dove into greasy pig pits, ran manic *cochons de lait*, and donned bird beaks and corn silk wigs. Women leapt over boiling pots of crawfish and crowned their heads with glistening king cakes. At first, the mêlée seemed no more alarming than Mardi Gras. Everyone was someone else; everyone was a figment. Before long, though, the carnival upended. Beaks turned into snouts, cakes turned into sow's ears, and hair fell out like fur. Finally, the feasters became meat, as the delirious Sabines spun on their own spits roasted by the strangers, who shed their gentleman's masks, and they looked too late at the saw-tooth faces of the real *tatailles*, the oil tycoons who now laid claim to their swampland and to the glistening black pools under their feet.

Late one night, after I turned thirteen, marks appeared on my skin like a sudden rash. By then, there was talk in Louisiana about the damage of the oil derricks, all the sulfur and minerals drilled out of the ground and into the air. Industrial silos rose up all around us, issuing smoky gray clouds like uneasy brain lobes that hung in the sky longer than any thunderstorm. The bayou water took on a sick look, too, with a bilious green that oozed like a running sore. Water needs to breathe, everyone said through tight lips. All the talk was of an evil poison. Over a stretch of Cajun country, in a crescent-shaped alley, cancer blossomed like kudzu in lungs, in stomachs and colons, in glands and tissues with names no one could pronounce. Tumors, seizures, fits that got chalked up to the nerves, and odd skin rashes.

Yet mine wasn't a rash. Instead, like my outlaw grandfather, I was a vein-hunting warrior, only I wanted to let the juice out not in, let it burn not cool. In a fever dream, a thick line of twisting blossoms crept over my arms as if the nerves beneath were flowering. One tiny bud opened in my hand, in the crook where a pen would go. Others burst open in radiating zigzag lines. A little cluster of roses, each a shade darker than the next. The petals grew blurry at the edges with an anxious halo. To no good end, I burned each mark into the skin with the cherry glow of a cigarette. The ash raised the hairs then turned them black before the ember raised a scarlet ring and a plume of sulfur reached my nose.

As smoke rose around me, hot words filled my head, hot names too. A pack of boys in roper boots had gotten my scent that year. I smelled of flowery cologne and fruity hairspray. I smelled of sweet mouthwash and pretty soap. Growing deaf to Mama, I flipped up my collar and feathered my hair. I scrunched up my sleeves and flashed a wristband. I double-looped a knot in my belt. First year in high school, I pushed against my uniform. The pack of boys delivered warnings with their eyes. In the gym, they curled lips, flared nostrils, stamped heels. At recess, they swaggered and swore. In fluorescent hallways, they thrust out their tongues like a wedge of swans to imitate my speech. Then, in unlit bathroom stalls, they shoved their hands in my pants, shoved their fingers in my face. After school, they fed their knuckles to my mouth. I swallowed it all, the oily saliva, the fleshy blood, the feverish words and hot hot names.

Yet I badly wanted to shift shape. I wanted to flick a magic finger in the air like my papère, to make buildings explode, to gnash teeth, crunch bones. I wanted to stretch my neck and soar through the clouds. So I leapt from the roof of Divine Redeemer, with birds singing in my ear and lights flashing in my eyes, until I crashed and crunched my own bone—a fractured femur. Just a dizzy ballerina, the boys said, a flightless fairy.

Still, the pain shook me into relief. After that, I burnt my arms again and again with a cigarette, burnt my chest too. I started slapping my head with my hands, snapping my wrist with a rubber band. Then I drew a finger across the edge of a steak knife. Something in me wanted out, so I punctured a vein. No matter how hard I tried, I never shifted shape. I never became a champion of any kind. I never fought that pack of boys, never even tried to outrun them. Instead, when cornered and faced with another meaty fist, I opened my mouth and closed my eyes, ready for the tongue of fire, the revelation of names. Ready to eat words, swallow blood. Ready for the lesson, the chokehold of redemption.

Late in his life, when I met my papère, he'd lost all speech. All words had left him. He grunted, and his wife brought him a can of *pop rouge* with a bent straw. He groaned, and his sons smacked his remaining leg while the phantom one seemed to shiver. He wore dark sunglasses, even inside, like a mask over his eyes. If he could've spoken, what would the outlaw have said to his grandson? Would he have greeted him as a fellow rebel, a renegade fairy? If he had both legs, would he have raised the sissy-boy onto his shoulders and paraded him through town, shouting his pride in French? Or would he have slipped off his belt to deliver a carnal blessing?

Late, very late at night, in my own version of the Sabine story, my werewolf papère stands at the mouth of the den, fending off all predators. We may be hungry, our tongues may be sickly white, but when a basket of food appears, my grandfather lifts a leg over it, sprays, and kicks it away. He stands his ground and keeps constant watch for any change in the air, any sudden noise or movement. His eyes are black as bayous. From rocks, he draws water, clean and clear. From dirt, he pulls cakes, sweet and moist. From his neck, an endless chain of zigzag teeth swings like a second jaw. He moves without caution and knows no taboo. He'd frighten any tataille into the woods, chase any pack of animals into the dark. He'd terrify the words out of any boy's mouth, chew the mask off any villain's face. Yet his breath is perfume. At midnight, with his long tongue, he licks the wounds on my skin until they seal and form gray scabs. In the morning, he clicks them each with his champion toe and the scabs fall off. A shock goes through me, and my face breaks into a troubled smile. All around, the smell of roses.

II.

ACCOUNTS OF
THE RECKONING

"As the Acadians became Cajuns then Cajun-Americans, they began to lose their words and ways: forgetting the French word for the thing in their hand or fixing crawfish étouffée from a can. Yet the music, they kept that. They kept the fiddle too, but now they played with split-tongue harmonicas and push-button accordions, and they sang in English with hard lyrics and a manic pace. The change in tempo and words made them no difference, long as they could play. Still, something was lost. Maybe for good. One thing's for certain: that language is gonna die. All the gumbo ya-ya of Cajun talk is dying. Soon, there'll be no one alive with that tongue. And I ask you: how will we receive Communion then?"

— Beausoleil Canard on KJUN Radio

"If the swamp was whiskey and I was a duck,
I'd dive to the bottom and take me a suck.
But, hey, I ain't no duck,
So, c'mon buzzard and pick,

Pick a hole in this sad old lonesome head.
Pick, buzzard, pick
Keep on picking 'til I'm dead."

— "Acadian Two-Step"
Louis "La La" Lejeune

8.

FATHER FOX

"Don't tell anyone," he said, before he told me the story.

My father's tales starred cheats, thieves, and priests, and he figured at thirteen I was old enough to hear one of his favorites. It began like this: once he knew a long-nosed priest who got bounced from so many parishes that he wore running shoes instead of clerical loafers. *Père Renard*, or Father Fox, as the kids called him, operated church bingo like a game of casino craps, barking out numbers and taking much more than petty change as bets. At the end of a good night, he might walk out with a wad of sawbucks, a set of cast-iron pots, the keys to a riding lawn mower, and a couple of roosting chickens, to boot.

Father Fox never got busted for the bingo, though. What arrested him in the end hung from both arms. That priest possessed a magic set of hands, the kind that could sink anything in the soil—a sorry-looking seed, a dried-up root, or an old bulb from a dead plant—only to watch it sprout overnight like a Cajun version of Jack and the Beanstalk. Lilies at Easter, of course, irises too. Marigolds, crêpe myrtles, even a magnolia tree. Yet another plant raised a stink, a tall thin weed with leaves like tangled palms. Ladies in mantillas fanned themselves to a fury when they heard the priest not only grew marijuana behind the rectory but sold it to their teenagers through the lattice of the confessional.

After the word spilled on his unholy church business, rumors filled the air about Father Fox and his long-fingered hands, which possessed another kind of magic. Those ten fingers divined their way into the purses of older women and the pants of younger boys. During Mass, heads nodded as he broke the sacred host but not in reverence for the liturgy. As my father put it, all those lace-headed ladies nodded in disbelief. Who had let *un renard fou* out of another troubled house and into their own den? When would the bishop or the pope strip his black cassock right off him?

Father Fox just sniffed at the air with his long nose and ignored the birds circling overhead. He blamed the gossip on the idle words of another priest, another parish. Or he shrugged away the rumors like any false merchant or true politician. One of his favorite quotes came not from the Bible but from Louisiana's longest-running governor, a man who also might be found at a game of craps.

"The only way I can lose," he boasted before election season or a court session, "is if they catch me in bed with a live boy or a dead girl."

In the end, that governor got nabbed in a casino scheme then sent to the coop, while the priest got trapped in a drug sting then bounced free after a call to the bishop. Parishioners claimed even if Father Fox got nailed to a cross, he'd hotfoot his way to freedom and a profit. Hell, he'd sell tickets to his own wake, stuff his coffin with loot from the rectory, play poker with the devil, fault God for any debt, and still take bets on his resurrection. After all, if anyone knew the wages of sin, it was a priest.

As my father finished the story, he slammed his beer down, opened his mouth wide and let loose a wild howl of laughter.

"DON'T TELL ANYONE," HE said as he opened the door.

"Forgive me, Father, for I have sinned," I said in a hush. My voice sounded singsong, birdlike, even in my ear, as I hesitated at the threshold of the confessional. The priest was on the wrong side of the booth, the side where the penitent would enter. Where would I sit? Where would I kneel?

"Don't tell anyone," the priest said again, as he held out a hand to muzzle my mouth. His black cassock parted to expose a crooked pant leg. His fingers stretched in the air while that leg shifted. In the dark of the booth, the velvet curtain whispered and the wood bench whined. The gruff voice of the priest grunted in my ear, and his eyes blazed before mine. "A secret," he commanded, tapping his shoe on the floor. Then one more sound: a zipper. His hand pulled me to his waist, fingers slipped into my mouth. The cassock tangled up in his pants, and he crouched to step out of it, like an animal shaking off an extra skin. His long nose sniffed at the air around me.

What I had to confess: impure thoughts, lust for other boys, nightly self-abuse. I let a boy yank down my pants and rub against me under the bleachers, it was true, I locked lips with a yearbook picture of the football star and prayed he'd lay me on the field, I lingered in the gym shower until my skin turned red and the boy at my back tugged off then turned away, and I laughed aloud at the word "homo," as if it was the punch line to a joke not aimed at me.

In the confessional, though, there was no punch line, no joke. There was only a half-naked priest with furry red patches and yellow eyes daring me to leave the booth, betting I'd stay. "A secret," he repeated. His eyes shone like mirrors, as if waiting for me to drop to my knees like a real penitent. Did he count on me to play along because he was holy? Because I was homo? By thirteen, I knew how the story went. I'd learned the theater of church and the gamble of faith. I'd learned to take the host between my teeth, to let it sit on my tongue and let it melt there. I'd learned to genuflect, to kneel, and to pray for a reason to kneel. And I'd learned once already the hard blessing of a priest's hand on my legs, the heat of false mercy and the fire of mean grace. That other priest had opened his arms in the confessional too, had held a finger to his mouth, then pointed that same finger in catechism, joking with the boys about my swishing hips, my flapping hands and stammering lips. A secret, I understood, was a cross. Sooner or later, you were nailed to it and the only way free was down.

So when the priest sunk into his chair and parted his legs, at first I rose. My back arched and my shoulders widened, while I lowered my mouth down to his waist, shut my lips tight, and summoned my own kind of magic. He jerked his hips and grabbed my ears as I sank lower and lower, my face buried in his skin. Then a light burst in my eyes, and I rose up again. My arms spread to the walls, wide as wings, my head scraped the vault, high as a hawk, my mouth split open and I finally answered him with a loud and sharp tongue.

"One may keep a secret," I said, "but not two."

He opened his jaw, flashed his teeth and sank back on his legs, as if to leap up, but my mouth split open again and this time I said, "No need to tell anyone what everyone already knows."

Suddenly, the priest gekkered and gasped before his nose shriveled into his face, and his fingers drew into his hands, and his arms and legs grew smaller and smaller in the confessional, small enough that his whole body fit on the kneeling rail. From there, he bowed his head and offered to sell his lush fur for a pardon, his lavish tail for a prayer. Then he reversed himself and denied all sin, calling out accusations and excuses in a low growl, his tongue a flame of fire. It was the true beast, it was the false lamb, he said, it was *not* him. He faulted his red pelt, his sharp teeth, and his curled fingers. He faulted his long pointed nose and the odd perfume of boys. He faulted his tongue and the maker of his tongue until his voice hoarsened into a howl empty of all words, just a choking sound and a dimming echo.

In the end, the priest disappeared in a foam of yeast and wheat, a desecrated host. Through the lattice of the door, a terrific peal of thunder rang over the pews into the organ of the choir room. The pipes bellowed the chords to a hymn sung for the Fraction of the Eucharist. I ran first toward the sound and the light raining through the stained-glass windows then out of the church and into the empty parking lot before saliva shot across my teeth and I spat a medallion, shiny and round, in a crack of pavement. In that spot, a lily shot up, a stargazer with gold filaments, a bright orange stigma, and a crown of purple petals. At last the church bells marked the hour, and I headed home with a fire in my chest, a new story in my head, and a wild chorus of laughter rising in my wake.

9.

MOST HOLY GHOST

Down in the tail of the parish, where the bayou emptied all its secrets, I grew certain my grandfather lurked, waiting for me to find him. Since I'd only met him once before he disappeared, the odds were long that I'd ever catch his scent or follow his trail. Yet by thirteen, I was hell-bent to try.

Unlike most men in Acadiana, my papère claimed neither a medieval French name nor legal standing in any court. No paper certified his birth, no deed titled his property, and no child carried his name. He harvested no crop, from the land or the gulf, and never carried a wallet, much less cash. Sabine not Cajun, Pentecostal not Catholic, he stood on the other side of any wall. Yet for a while, as part-time minister and full-time traiteur, Rex held a world in his hands. He controlled the revival tent and the medicine cabinet. He ruled the roost and the range, cooking up food and faith in the same cast-iron skillet. He knew no rules and saw no reason to stay on one plot of land or in one kind of body.

His legend filled my head as I grew up, from the stories Mama told me at night. His restless eyes saw further than any man's; his wild hair ran longer than any woman's. His skin was dark as roux and rough as cypress. From Mama, I heard how he could raise a soufflé in the kitchen of a moving train and a spirit in the body of a half-dead man. From others, I heard how he could lift the blood in any woman and a flaming dove in the air. Then too, he could lie with steady eyes and summon hell on the dance floor with a fiddle under his chin.

In tale after tale, he'd vanish through the Vermilion into the mouth of the gulf only to shift shape and reappear in a new body. One time: with a crew cut and clipped nails, he surfaced reed thin, clean-shaven, atop a gray mare. Another time: with a bushy ponytail and brawny arms, he showed a beard down his chest and trailed a mangy bluetick coonhound. Every time: a cloud of mist rose about him, the kind that blurred the horizon at the marsh and made dawn look like dusk.

To hear people tell it, my grandfather was a one-man band. His skin was a leather drum; his lungs were accordion bellows.

He made music with nothing but a single cattail and a set of wet lips. What's more, he wrestled a brown bear for breakfast and barbecued a green gator for lunch. He raised a wood-shingled home on the bayou in less than a month and took it down with hot breath and a match in one day. Afterwards, he slept in a duck blind—or claimed to—hunted from a *pirogue*, and was seen indoors only if there was an open bar under the roof. The Last Outlaw, they called him.

The tales of Rex were sometimes comic, always strange. Once, a jealous woman paid him to toss a bag of *gris-gris* at Missy Possum's Parlor of Beauty & Sociability. Prone to excess in everything, by the light of a full moon Rex covered the entire front porch of the little tin shack with gutted and plucked black chickens, plus thirteen bags of stinkweed. After cleaning the mess all the next morning, Missy set about rinsing, rolling, and drying her clients' hair. But when the towels were lifted, two of the women found themselves as bald as the chickens that Rex had hung from the porch, while one was left with a green tint on her hair no amount of bleach could lift or dye could cover. The green-haired woman kept asking everyone in sight how such a grand tataille could be let out of his cage. She seemed shocked that any man could find his way to a beauty parlor, much less tell the difference between peroxide and bleach, dye and lye. Yet the two bald women expressed no surprise at all. Each was already well-acquainted with Rex's voodoo spells, being joined with him still in a state of holy—and apparently illegal—matrimony.

When the deputy arrived with a warrant at Rex's front porch, it took three men, a fishing net, and a tow bar from a pick-up truck to haul him away. The women each raised an open mouth to the sky, sure this time he'd been nailed for good. Down at the station, though, the cops swore the net arrived with nothing but the smell of briny shrimp and empty pink shells. In the middle of the sea foam, there was a hind claw with a bit of meat stuck to it, though no one could say what kind.

Maybe that story, and the others, were meant as postcards from a world losing air. A world where living food petrified, untouched, and dying music echoed, unheard. If light was fading on Cajun men, it had burnt out—utterly and completely—on their darker kin, the mixed-blood Sabines, who only lived in folklore now. The Sabine legend was a gray monument razed by time, and my Sabine grandfather was left a relic. The more time accelerated, the more bizarre the stories ran, the more impossible and the less credible. The less holy too. Who could have faith in a man charged with befoulment of beauty parlor water? Who could worship a giant man dragged away by three cops and a tow bar before shrinking to the size of a shrimp and slipping out to sea? Who could believe in a half-French, half-Indian, all-powerful man who had finally and fully vanished, leaving not so much as a footstep or a fingerprint?

Or maybe the stories were cautionary tales. Don't-turn-out-like-that tales. After all, from my grandparents' time to my parents', both Cajuns and Sabines had turned themselves from one kind of people into another, speaking English instead of French, buying food from a shelf, clothes from a rack, leaving bayous and farms for cities and towns, counting bills in a wallet instead of points on a buck. Most practiced the same religion in the same church, but with less fervor and a low fire. Even then, they had to accept a new creed and throw off an old one, and they had to watch for the odd yearling with its head turned around backward.

The oldest faith Mama knew was in Rex. She'd seen him only half a dozen times since he was dragged away from her childhood, but she kept vigil every Sunday. Even though she pledged Catholic to marry a pure Cajun, for years Mama tuned into the *Most Holy Ghost Revival Hour* before donning a mantilla for high noon mass. She clapped her hands like thunder and shouted a line or two of gospel, while letting her head snap from side to side. In those Pentecostal moments, she dropped the stern forehead, the worrisome brow. Her hair remained a dark corona yet her whole face brightened. Either she summoned the past or warded it off, I couldn't tell which, but what seemed old and familiar to her looked new and fantastic to me. You could clap yourself into a spell? You could chant yourself into a whole other self?

Soon as the *Most Holy Ghost Revival Hour* ended, Mama shut it off with a determined click. Then she fixed one last bobby pin to the lace on her head, and fixed her face into the look of a Catholic parishioner.

Divine Redeemer, with its severe steeple and bishop's throne, only ran by one script, with no claps and no chants and no one turning into anyone else. It had pipe organ music, no rocking choir, and the priests wore starchy gowns and stiff lace, not open collar shirts and belted trousers. Everyone ate pressed wafers and drank grape juice and walked in straight, orderly lines and sat in straight, orderly pews. No one, not one person, sweated. No one fell out of a seat or spoke a single word, except on cue and in unison.

"See," Mama said, "How you look matters."

I knew what she meant: the pews up front bore brass plaques with the names of attorneys, surgeons, politicians, and farm bureau chiefs. Men who ran the city and the parish, all of Acadiana and at least this part of Louisiana. All Catholic, Mama reminded me, and all in their pews every Sunday. No Pentecostal ever sat in the mayor's seat. No Sabine ever rode on the king's float at Mardi Gras. Not even my grandfather, not even with a name like Rex.

Mama nudged me into those lines, pressed my white jackets, knotted my blue ties, creased my short pants, and polished my black shoes. She combed my hair, sometimes ironing out stubborn curls with a hot clamp. Whether inside the Catholic church or outside the Catholic school, I looked ready for an official First Communion photo, even at the age of thirteen. All her grooming brushed away the Sabine, the coppery reds that ran from my papère to her to me. Maybe I had none of my own father's ashy blond hair, but—when kept out of the sun—my skin lightened enough to pass for full-blooded Cajun. Still, I knew I didn't fit my skin, knew I was no straight, orderly Catholic boy.

Early one Sunday, Mama got a long distance call and pulled not just the receiver but the entire phone with its coiling cord into the bathroom, where her sobs rang out against the porcelain and the chrome and the beveled mirror.

"Gone?" was all I could hear her ask, "How could he be gone? Gone gone gone?"

She stayed in the bathroom the rest of the morning, with water running and running, and I walked paces outside the door. Long after she put down the receiver, Mama kept talking in half-sentences and broken thoughts. At times, her voice sounded muzzled with a towel then it exploded into a long chain of moans. Just before noon, the knob turned and she stepped out with a different face, her brows more arched, her lips more drawn, and her eyes a blaze of shadow and light. She stood still for a moment with only her fingers shaking at her side. I wanted to link my hand in hers, but she looked past me to the opposite wall. A picture hung there, her father in his Sunday revival finest, clutching a Bible in one hand and a set of beads in the other. His hair and skin glistening with sweat.

Right then, in the unlit hall without a radio or record playing, Mama raised her mouth to the ceiling and sang out loud. She clapped the beat then shouted the chorus to "I Married Jesus" and "He's Got the Whole World in His Hands." As her voice rose higher, the specter of her father rose out of that picture and into the air before us, thin and gray and only barely visible. With Mama's voice rattling the air, he jigged a leg and waved a stick to beat time. He didn't look at either one of us. He just stared straight ahead, like a dead-eyed bogeyman. Yet he shook with secret life. For all I knew, if Mama touched his ghostly body, he might explode into song—just like that—with a flame dancing over his head.

Instead, he disappeared from the hall soon as Mama stopped singing and closed the door to her bedroom. When I looked back at the picture, my papère hadn't moved, but the beads snaked around his hand now, and the Bible had cracked open, and his shoes hovered above the ground.

After that, the *Most Holy Ghost Revival Hour* fell out of rotation in our house, and Mama fell out of clapping and shouting and even sometimes fell out of high noon mass. The house seemed to fill with invisible figures, and the church seemed to shrink everybody to a dot in an infinite line. Mama's late-night tales stopped, and the TV grew louder in the living room, with laugh lines and canned applause, followed by breaking news and urgent forecasts. Papa worked in an oil refinery until long past dusk, ate from a cellophane-wrapped bowl Mama left in the microwave, then headed for his garage of solitude to sink his hands into a car engine or lawn mower.

At first, I performed my own disappearing act, into book after book, eating the pages for dinner, for lunch, for breakfast.

Then I conjured my own tales of Rex. I mussed my hair in the mirror, loosened my tie and clapped my head with my hands, twisting my hips and singing to a transistor and the back of a brush. When no one burst through the door and whipped me with a belt, when no one hauled me by my hair to kneel on the kitchen floor, when no one—meaning Mama, only Mama—let loose a hot line of Holy Scripture over my head, I took it as a sign and shook all caution from my body. Crossing one leg over the other at the knee, dangling a wrist in the air.

Finally, I performed my own first spell as I rose out of Mama's closet, wearing a cameo brooch on a belted jacket and a cloud of mousse in my freshly dyed hair. I kept my chin steady, or tried to, as I walked under the octopus-armed chandelier and across the shag carpet. The air was insulated with cotton, and all the furniture sat motionless, as if no one had sat down or stood up all day. Every surface of the house acted like a seal, letting not a single sound loose. Then I slid out a high-backed chair and took my place at the dinner table.

All at once, the silence not only broke but my mother's hands flew at me. Her hands shook and clapped again and again, on my head, on my hot cheeks, on my neck and arms and legs and up and down my back, as I rolled onto the ground and she shouted a streak of words ripped not from the Bible or any book I knew. The words smoked and steamed and rattled and burst around us until the TV sounded a news alert and the holy breath left my mother's chest in heavy clouds. After each breath,

I thought I heard her cry a name, her father's name. That night, I awoke while walking in the middle of the hall, saying his name myself. What did either of us think he could do? What kind of prayer was his name?

If he'd been sitting at the dinner table when I twirled into view, Rex might've clapped his big paw on my back to welcome a fellow changeling, a fellow outlaw. Yet for unending days after, my mother wrung her hands and worried over a scourge even her holy father could never heal. He'd become a ghost, but her son was more haunting. Sure, her father had poisoned a beauty parlor and shifted his shape right out of her life, but her son dyed his own hair and painted his own face—along with the nails on his hand. Black eyeliner, black nails. And what kind of voodoo was that?

Afterward, I witnessed Mama's own shape-shifting, even more than it had before. She straightened her hair with fuming chemicals and ironed the stray curls around her ears. She avoided the sun, smeared a pale cream on her face, and rinsed her hair with lemons. She hung up her dotted cotton dresses and closed-toe shoes, and wore belted pantsuits, cork-wedged sandals, and a silk headband. Her neck grew longer, like a swan, and the few dresses she wore rose well above her ankle now. She dangled a cigarette from her lips and a few swear words too. She still flared her nostrils when I smudged ash on my eyelids, but she let me dress myself for school, for church, let me aim her hot dryer at my hair until it ran wild. Soon, her gospel albums were shelved, and she spun New Orleans funk on the turntable at night, singing the nonsense lyrics out loud while she waved her hands to the ceiling. During one song, she raised a fist and punched at the space where my father should've been dancing. Where some man should've been dancing.

Other times, though, she'd drop the diamond needle on a record, and her feet would come to life. A woman's blue voice, gravelly and low or crystalline and high, testified about her troubles, and Mama rocked along—leg to leg and hip to hip—until her hands found their way to the kitchen where the healing happened.

She couldn't summon her father back home, I knew, couldn't raise his spirit anymore. Now that he was gone, there was no holy fire left. Yet with the crack of an egg and the twirl of a spoon, she whipped up a chiffon pie, a sheet of pecan pralines, a row of cream-filled éclairs. Or else beignets light as air. She knew every one of her *père*'s tricks in the kitchen, how to stir a gumbo without ruining the roux, how to cook a root to cure the flu, how to raise pockets of dough into hallowed pastries and holy clouds of powdered sugar. In the late afternoon, with the waning sun, with my father still away at work, Mama served gold-lined plates of treats to her only son. Any trespass was forgiven, any penance forgotten. Her every move in the kitchen was a religious rite. And I would lift my ears, listening to her tell stories and recite recipes, converted by each word into her apostle. The whole world had shrunk for her, I could see. The distance was short between a meal and a memory, but over time it also got shorter between grace and grievance. On the right rare night, Mama's delicate fingers placed a gold-lined plate of goodies before my father too, and his face beamed with light.

She conducted other kinds of healing. A soft pass with a cayenne poultice over my arm sealed a wound or erased a bruise, a gentle press on my forehead with a kerosene cloth lifted a rash or settled my nerves. When she told a wild joke or a madcap story, clouds of powdered sugar moved through the air like healing ghosts.

It was all a confection, her faith, and any shift in the ingredients could make it rotten or sweet. A phantom father. A make-believe husband, a son in make-up. A holy song no longer sung. Or a copper sheet filled with cut-out shapes and a cast-iron skillet lifted over a fire. She was her father's daughter but had her own secret name: Evangeline. She was the only heir to his power and the only testament to his legend. Crescent-shaped pastries, half-moon cookies, shell-shaped cakes, and there it was: a whole world in her hands.

10.

BLACK SHEEP BOY

Like a morgue, no matter the blistering pavement or the bulb red temperature outside, the classroom remained a cold chamber. Windows frosted inside with tiny stalagmites of ice rising around the edges. Books stiffened like frozen meat and made slapping sounds when the covers shut. And chairs all stuck in place, screwed down by the alabaster man in front of the room.

"Morphodites and Bedlamites," our junior-year English teacher shouted over the heads of the class, while a cloud of white smoke billowed out of his mouth.

Mr. Hedgehog, as we called him, was a prickly short-limbed monster who wore a frock coat no matter the weather and wielded a baton like the conductor of a manic orchestra. He brought the baton down on our essays as if they were hideous scores of sheet music. He beat on the covers of books as if they were hidebound drums. More than once, he beat on the back of a pupil's hand. Then, lightning quick, he'd snap out the words: "Just a love tap!" His tongue practically hissed against his teeth.

Before we were born, he often told us, before we were "dirty thoughts in our dirty parents' minds," our city had been the site of famous riots, with fire hoses, street bombs, and bloodhounds. At the start of one long hot summer, "the Blacks just rose up," he said, "and the South fell down."

He taught English but rewrote history with every book we read. His baton slapped my desk and sometimes slapped my hand too when I corrected a fact or a date. About the riots, he had the year right, but the city and state were wrong—and there was something else wrong too. He spoke the word "Black" as if it was the sound you made at the first bite of a wretched meal.

During exams, he paced the aisles with his baton, bringing it down on the head of the student who reached for an eraser or a bottle of whiteout. He saw any answer but the first as evidence of cheating and any stray ink on the page as evidence of guessing, more vile than cheating. He saw closed eyes as the work of moles and crossed-out words as the mark of worms. He saw errors in us all and even foresaw our end, as he put it, "scratching out the days like birds on a shrinking shore." What exactly he meant, we couldn't figure out, except that it sounded like the last line of a novel. Maybe one he wrote? Like a lot of our teachers, he hated teaching, hated especially teaching his subject and dropped reminders of his once promising writing career before the Great Sacrifice he made for us all. He trusted no book and told us how every author got it all wrong except one. Dizzy with opium and teenage girls, with salty air and sailors, with jazz and martinis, with gunpowder and arms, every American writer wrote a pack of lies, he said, except the one who came on like a liar—with a fake name and the full costume of a fake Southern gentleman. When we read the *Only* Great American Novel, our teacher fondled the ribbon tie he wore and, at each dramatic plot twist, brought one of the tips into his mouth for punctuation.

"Can't depend on nobody but your slave," he told us when we reached the sidewinder ending. "That, *mes enfants*, is the moral."

When I raised my hand with a correction, he delivered a sharp love tap to my knuckles with his baton and said, "Not this time, smarty pants. This time you let it stand or dance those prissy feet right back to the counselor's office!"

No else said a word, frozen in their seats, frozen in time, so I let my hand fall. In the next row, another student sat stiff but angled his head around to look me dead in the eye. Boogie, the sole senior in our class, almost never looked up from his desk and never raised a hand. Yet on the field, his wide hands tore through the air to catch pass after pass and run play after play. "Best Offensive Player in Acadiana" the papers said, "Best Running Back in Louisiana. He had another title on campus too: "Best All-Around Black." Black and white students sat in the same class but on different student councils and for different award ceremonies, long after that long hot summer and long long after Reconstruction. To most, that was just a fact, no question. So when Boogie wouldn't pose with his Best All-Around Black trophy, the other students chalked it up to vanity.

"Too big a star for us already, Boogie," they teased, but our teacher put it another way.

"Maybe he's holding out for valedictorian," Mr. Hedgehog said. "Now that'd be a plot twist!" Then he clapped the air in applause.

Boogie was barely passing English, barely passing all his classes, even though, rumor had it, his college test scores set a campus record. Teachers constantly found him dozing in his seat—when he showed—or drawing odd shapes instead of writing answers for fill-in-the-blank exams. For multiple choice or true/false, Boogie placed an X in every box, and for essays, he wrote with backward letters in a cursive hand that caused our English teacher to wrinkle his nose.

"Give a jock a pen," Mr. Hedgehog said, "and he uses it like a rip saw."

When he taught Civics, his other subject, he called us "miscreants and reprobates" and pronounced "civilization" like it was a congenitally contracted disease. Close contact with Mr. Hedgehog, we were sure, would be worse than any STD. He'd leave you bloody with quills.

WE WERE RIDING ACROSS the Atchafalaya Basin, Boogie and me, down one of the longest bridges in the world, eighteen miles of concrete rising over muddy swamp. The water below looked nearly black, but it was covered in patches with a green overgrowth that looked like the hide of some prehistoric creature. Through the patches, tall gray trees rose up, bald and spiny, the skeletons of a day when cypress was cut down like reeds. They looked like old debutantes, those trees, with their branches spread out for a waltz and their trunks arranged in billowing rows of pleats. The whole picture was frozen in time, except for the quivering nose of the car and the quick tongue of the running back next to me. For that moment, I had no idea where we were headed and little idea of where we'd been. As if the swamp itself gave us permission, we lifted right out of the car, right out of high school and the roles we played: the football star and the quiz kid, the stag and the fag.

Nearly dizzy from the night heat, I struggled to remember how Boogie ended up in my car. Already painted a Jenny Woman at school, I'd openly set my sights on studying the cheerleader stunts. During the game, I couldn't tell a route from a sweep, but I knew every step of an arabesque. All season, I followed our football team to away games, this time to a school in Assumption Parish in a town called Confederate. I secretly hoped to join the cheerleaders, to sit on the bus next to the players and their broad backs and wide grins. In the locker room, I might've been taunted for the direction of my eye, but in the bleachers I could stare openly at the boys in padded shoulders and tight lace-up pants. And when they lifted each other off the ground or delivered slaps to backs and rear ends, I could throw my hands together with the cheerleaders and yell each player's name out loud.

After the game in Confederate, I'd sat at a red light, yards behind the school bus, while tumbles and twirls ran through my head and a circle of players huddled before my eyes. Without warning, the passenger door opened and Boogie sat down beside me. He said not a word. He just looked straight ahead until the light turned green.

On the long drive back, he pumped me with questions, and to each one, I lied. Yes, I drank every lewd shot he could name. Yes, I smoked this, snorted that. Yes, I yanked it in the lockers, in the bleachers. Yes, I'd nailed a girl, nailed her good, nailed her again and again. I hadn't done any of it, not yet, but I knew the signs of a test, and I knew how to score an A. Still, I didn't know where the test would end. Suddenly, Boogie looked me in the eye and asked, "Ever stick it in a guy?"

I stammered and pretended to look at traffic, not ready to switch on the truth.

"A guy ever stick it in you?"

My eyes stared at the school bus ahead, and my tongue thickened.

"Ain't any different," he said. "A hole is a hole."

The words hit the windshield and burst like fruit. No one had ever talked to me like Boogie, like I was another player on the field. His talk made my ears burn and my head throb, but his voice wasn't the only one I heard. All around, I heard the furious sound of pent-up laughter. The laughs slipped out of the cracked windows of the school bus ahead, crammed with the rest of the football team, the pep squad, and the cheerleaders. The players rose and fell in shadows against the window with pantomime movements and quick jerking arms. The cheerleaders beat time with their gloved hands, and the pep squad opened their mouths in unison. They looked like they were cheering Boogie and me from the back of the bus, but I knew they weren't. Already the rumors were starting, already the talk was hitting the air like splinters of glass, clear and piercing. What was Boogie doing with that fag?

I opened my mouth and laughed, a tinny nervous laugh. Boogie laughed along, his eyes shining like copper pennies in a fire. Did either of us know what the hell we were doing together?

To avoid any more of his questions, I started asking Boogie some of my own. Why didn't he talk in class? I'd seen him write down an answer when Mr. Hedgehog called a question, but Boogie never spoke it out loud. Why?

"Don't play by the rules," he said, "when the game is rigged."

"But what about your grade?" I asked.

"Got that in the bag."

"How?"

For a moment, Boogie fell silent, his face set in concentration. Whether from the stadium bleachers or the seat next to him, his sturdy body looked built for the game, built for running, catching, and tackling men on a wide field. Yet up close his face looked delicate, like a guy about to play a cornet, with a shadow around his eyes and a worry on his lips. Did he have the breath ready? The notes right?

"Oh, I'll pass," he said, almost in a whisper. "Wanna see my study guide?"

I gripped the steering wheel and nodded yes. What would he show me?

THE BAR WAS NAMED after one of its lewd shots: Between the Sheets. Only everybody called it Sheets. "Don't skid the Sheets," I heard one guy say to a burst of laughter—before a cloud of silence moved overhead. Once Boogie passed through the door, a hand went up in my direction, palm forward. Then a string of eyes lit up, feet spread, and nostrils flared. No one said a word, but I heard them clearly. "What is it you want?" Drinks rattled in glasses, and a funk song throttled the floor. "What is it you want, white boy?"

Suddenly, I wasn't just the fag. I wasn't just the queer quiz kid. Here, I was white before all. Even with the red flashes of

Sabine skin, even with the wild bush of hair, I wasn't black. At Sheets, there were only two options, no choice, the same as Boogie's award at school. Other people may have argued about prairie Cajuns and swamp Cajuns. Other people may have argued about pure French and Sabine French, Creole and mulatto, quadroon and octoroon. Here, there was no argument. Everything was clear as black and white, and I was the pink-eyed opossum in the room.

In the static of the moment, a hand on my shoulder jolted me into a chest-exploding gasp. When Boogie shouted "Boo" into my ear, and I jumped, the rest of the crowd laughed then turned back to pound the bar for more shots. "Slippery Nipple!" "Screaming Orgasm!" "Cocksucking Cowboy!" they hollered, and the names echoed in my head. Down at the end of the bar, Boogie introduced me as "little bro" and told everyone I was there to help with his studies. The guys in jerseys scoffed but looked at me as if a quiz kid might have some use after all. *First time at Sheets, first time as "little bro,"* I thought. *What was next?*

Most of the guys towered over me, and their hair rose even higher in geometric shapes, flat tops, blunt sides, sharp tips, sometimes with angular lines cut through the hair and to the scalp. Or else their hair fell in a sheen of loose curls. The cloud of pomade filled my nose like musk, and I would've played little bro to any guy in the room. None of them laid a hand on me, though. None grabbed my shoulder. Instead, they barked at the girls in shiny spandex and chunky gold necklaces and grabbed at the air left in their path. Just past the bar, the dance floor filled with couples jerking hips to songs about freak-a-zoids, robots, and neutron bombs falling from the sky. The whole place shook when a growling singer commanded them to "tear the roof off the sucker" and hands testified when a voice shouted about a black First Lady, but the dance floor really turned to riot with a song about an atomic dog. All at once, everyone shouted "dogcatcher" and bared teeth at the mirror ball as if it was the moon. The glistening bodies and surging beats drove the heat way up until bottles exploded and the guys in jerseys rained forty-ounces of beer over Boogie's head, and I suddenly remembered they won, our team won, and Boogie's name would splash all over the papers again. With fiery eyes, he schooled everybody on his moves and boasted of going pro faster than any rookie in history. His voice roared in a way it never did in class, and his hands looked wider than ever as they arced the air. Right then, I wanted to be the hips jerking next to him, the knees dropping to the floor, and the feet twisting into the ground. I wanted to be his freak-a-zoid little bro.

Instead, I was the hands on the wheel leaving the bar, taking directions from Boogie as the car winded through a neighborhood nearly as crooked as the bayou next to it. Lights from another car blazed in the rear view mirror then vanished before blazing again. Houses leaned in and out of view, most with a steep pitched roof and long galley porch. Then Boogie pointed his finger at the only Victorian house I'd seen in Lafayette, with millwork like tattered lace and a small domed doorway. On the steps, he grinned at me, and I grinned back. What would he show me now? At Boogie's first knock, a voice shouted *"Entrez"* and he pushed the door open with one hand. The night was hot and damp, but the house was cold and dry, with vents blowing from the floor. A single light clicked on at the end of the hall. Boogie walked straight ahead with sure steps, but I held back and eyed the street. When I heard the hum of a car engine, I slipped inside the house, feeling for the wall and blinking at the dark until my hands tipped over a coat rack. As I set it back, I could barely see the outline of a frock coat. I froze. Now I knew Boogie's study guide. It wasn't any spandex girl at Sheets and it wasn't ever to be me.

Down the hall, Boogie's hands flagged me toward an open door. His face beamed like a fugitive with a free boat and a way out. On the bed, a man's bare ass rose in the air, while a white silk nightshirt pooled around his face. *Could he see me?* I worried. *Could he see anything?* A chill had me rubbing my arms until Boogie laid his hand on my shoulder.

"You first," he said.

My hands dug deep into my pockets, and I shrank into my shoes then shook my head. So Boogie dropped his pants and jumped right onto the bed and right into Mr. Hedgehog, thrusting his haunches back and forth with his teeth bared and his head aimed at the ceiling. Outside, the moon shone like a disc of ice, white and cool and quiet. Yet inside, a grunting sound came from the bed, and it wasn't Boogie. The sheets were twisting and a set of hands were shaking and Mr. Hedgehog started to scream. A shrill sound tore out of his throat and rang overhead. In the window, a face eclipsed the moon. First one, then half a dozen guys in jerseys stared straight at the bed, straight at Boogie riding Mr. Hedgehog. They'd tailed us here, the football players, and now they crowded the window with flared eyes. Boogie didn't stop, though. He didn't see them, so he kept thrusting into our teacher while his teammates kept moving their mouths until a loud word rose up, then two: "Dog! Gay dog!"

At that, Boogie's head whipped down and caught sight of the players in the window. Suddenly, he was the dead-eyed guy in class again, wordless and blank. He slipped out of Mr. Hedgehog, slipped off the sheets and onto the floor. Then Mr. Hedgehog fell too, clawing at the air and gnashing his teeth. He tore a chunk off Boogie's shoulder and anointed his own skin with the blood. Then he curled into a ball and started moaning about headlines and reputation and a wrecked career.

Boogie's eyes flickered back to life, and he bolted down the hall, out the back door and hit the ground running. The players howled into the air, shaking the houses awake, then revved their car and left a hot streak on the road. I should've busted through the window and emptied my chest to the night. I should've torn the roof off the house and chased the players with a mad fury. I should've run after Boogie and hollered his name to the moon.

But I dropped to the floor and tucked tail, lower than any dog and stiffer than any opossum.

Yet when the cops showed, I found my feet and a story, however wrong or full of lies. I told them Mr. Hedgehog had lured me to his place with the promise of an A and a shot at a trophy. I told them he had pounced on me in his nightshirt and had shoved my face into a pillow. I told them he had a seizure in bed and had fallen to the floor. The teacher stayed silent as a corpse in a morgue. What could he say? That the promise went to a black boy? What could he do? Point his baton at the truth? No, he kept his thin lips shut while I told the cops my sidewinder of a story and Boogie ran free, with his long legs and his strong back leaving not a trace on the ground or a scent in the air.

Behind closed eyes, I followed his moves. He ran all the way down the street to the end of the bayou and right out of this city, right out of this state, right out of history, as far away as his feet could take him. Come winter, he wore a second hide, wrapped himself in a cloak of wool and slept under the northern lights. No one's dog, he studied the sky and redrew the constellations. No shepherd to heed, no flock to fold, he cut a crisscross path in the snow like a guide for the outlaw and the wayward, the outcast and the misfit. When I finally reached him, he shaded me in the sun, warmed me in the moon. Under his cloak, we lay together, and no one could tell the black sheep from the white or the field of stars from the dome of night.

11.

FEATHERS

The show was set to begin, signaled by strobe lights, smoke machines, and a red flasher lifted from a cop car. Feathers irritated the air as if in search of a head to dress or a sleeve to drape. Synthesizers accused the dancers of sin, and in answer they raised their hands up to the mirror ball. In a bar full of sweaty men and powder-faced boys, everyone wore a guilty face.

On a pillar near the makeshift stage, a poster announced memorial services for "our angel," a teenager who died at the end of a bat. In the picture, he was a slip of a girly boy with a slinky boa around his neck and a tilted fedora on his head. I recognized the face but not the painted-on beauty spot. He'd been in the class ahead of me and vanished from campus before the end of the term. Rumors flew in the air yet nothing landed in the papers, not even at school. He got called a lot of names in the locker room but never "angel." Unlike me, he didn't deny those names, even when bestowed with a fist. I should've spoken up, risen up, but I sank like an empty sack.

Now I wanted to trace his movements, so I headed to the bar where—rumor had it—the angel boy had performed. On my third night in a row, I sat staring at the poster, at that beauty spot, when a bartender's shaker banged against glass. The crack rang in my ear, and my body shook as if it'd been hit. One of the powder-faced boys offered me a whiff from an amber bottle. The chemical burn made my nose flare and my eyelids twitch, so the boy handed me a damp hankie and told me to hold it to my mouth and suck as if my ever-loving life depended on it.

"Spirits for the spirit," he said.

Once I huffed, my ears picked up sounds all around me. Through the blur, I could hear two queens conduct a trial for the angel boy's murder. One blamed a breeder, the other blamed rough trade, but both agreed the cops would never find the basher, would never try.

"When it comes to a dead queen," one said, "those pigs bury their head in the mud and lose all scent. Trust me, there will be no justice, *Mary*, and no mercy."

"Fuck mercy," the other declared, "This queen seeks vengeance."

Then the avenging queen turned his quiff my way with a proclamation.

"If one angel falls," he said, "another will rise."

After a deep huff on the bottle of poppers, I saw the vision in his eyes. He'd be that rising angel, his quiff streaked from a bottle of peroxide and a knit halter top stretched tight as cellophane against his breasts. He'd race out the bar with a pistol in hand. Jump in the open window of a white hatchback, throw the stick shift into gear. Speed through the gravel parking lot, take turn after turn as if his wheels were greased for the ride. He'd hang his head out the window, laugh at all the flat-chested boys. Weren't their nipples little pimple titties? Weren't theirs eraser-head tits? Weren't his tits better? They'd win him dates with the barback, the bartender, the bouncer. All the studs and gigolos on the sidewalk, all the ex-quarterbacks and jocks in the alley, wouldn't they stand back in amazement now, in absolute awe, for his surely were top-shelf, gold star, blue ribbon, head cheerleader, most-popular-boy-at-the-bar *breasts*. Before the crowd, he'd cock a gun in the air like a flaming blow dryer and shoot a turbo-charged inferno at any basher in the street who dared take a bat to a queen again.

The rush of the bottle left my head, and I saw the angel of vengeance as he now was: a petite wasp-waisted figure in a black velvet jacket. He looked right at me, tossed back a gold shot, then slapped a hand down on the worn oak.

"Senior year," he said, "that little angel never even finished school. Where's the mercy in that?"

He shook a hand at the ceiling before bringing it to his chest.

"In *my* senior year," the avenging angel said, cutting an exclamation mark in the air with his finger, "they voted me Most Likely to Suck Seed. Positively clairvoyant. After a couple of jocks delivered the award with their fists, I ended up with false teeth that pop out for a blow job. False tits would just complete the set."

He pointed toward his wigless head, a sign to call him *he*, he said, not *she*. He was en route to full-time *she* but didn't have the dough for a trip to Mexico and a pair of silicone pillows. Until then, she was only *she* when she made herself up.

"Miss Carriage," he extended his hand like a favor. "Some poor twinks think me gruesome, like I mean dead fetuses and weeping women. Get this straight: I do not mock women. No ma'am. I respect women. It's men I mock. Men in robes. Men in suits. Men in every costume they *drag* out of the closet."

His hand still graced the air. It seemed I should kiss it but he suddenly withdrew the offer. His nose flared and a yellow ring blazed around his gray eyes.

"The problem is these apolitical homos. They have no sense of justice, much less a miscarriage. Where's the justice when you get arrested for what you put in your mouth, honey? I ask you: is it *not* your own damn mouth?"

He answered himself with a "YES" that hissed in the air and stretched into two syllables.

"And where's the justice when you get bashed for what you put on your own face?"

Even though Miss Carriage was not made up, his eyebrows were plucked into commas and his lashes lengthened into quote marks. His hands were groomed too, with clear polish, so that every gesture shimmered in the black light. The tip of one finger drew an imaginary line up and down the bar.

"In Lafayette, these Cajun queens slip a De or a La into their name and think they're French aristocracy and thus *not* subject to sodomy laws, conduct codes, hateful bashers, or even—Goddess forbid—AIDS. The dizzy fools are heir to nothing, certainly not Stonewall, but they lord it over the joint with eyebrows supercilious and elbows akimbo. *Moi*, I'm not looking to rule nobody but myself."

He tossed back another gold shot.

"Teach, yes, but rule, no. And testify, always. I made that poster, and I will make these queens remember their history even if I have to shout it every night from the bottom of the urinal."

After hearing I was a junior at the high school where he graduated and where the latest angel disappeared, Miss Carriage announced that his Lady Cub Scout Class was officially in session. By the end of the night, he had warned me away from anyone in a uniform—whether cop or cleric—and had schooled me into a new vocabulary. Basket, bear, bottom, butch. Trick, trade, troll, twink. Each word had its own operating instructions. Breeder=Straight. Trade=Straight to Bed.

"Never turn trade for cash. Money cheapens everything, honey."

He narrowed his eyes and flared his nostrils.

"Get drugs instead. The only currency you can slam, smoke, sniff, snort, or shoot straight up your starfish."

Miss Carriage was older, nearly thirty, and the price for his tits had gotten bigger while his purse got smaller. At this point, he said he was just stuffing dreams down a crawfish hole, but as long as he was dreaming he might as well have the look of an angel—or a female private dick.

"Truth be told, I'm already a girl with a gun. And I see crime up and down this bar. Don't you?"

Miss Carriage never asked how I got into the bar (fake ID) or how many times I'd been (twice). He asked few questions he couldn't answer himself.

When my eyes finally turned back to the stage, a drag queen in a nun's habit held a paddle over a priest's rear end while four cowboys spurred imaginary horses and kicked their heels in unison singing "Bohemian Rhapsody."

"One of these days," Miss Carriage exclaimed, "I will work that stage over!"

"You don't perform?" I asked.

"Honey, every utterance is a performance. But if you mean lipsync for dear life before a dead mic to a set of musty show tunes, then the answer is a round NO. I've got better uses for this set of choppers."

A WEEK LATER, WE stood in a circle-shaped bar hidden under a huge cantilever bridge in the Louisiana state capitol. To get there, we had to drive over not one bridge but two, the first an endless ribbon of concrete running through murky swamp and the second a sky-high arch spanning the muddy Mississippi. A trip out of town, Miss Carriage had predicted, would shake up our spirits.

In the bar, a hulking drag queen named Miss Teary de la Place pushed around an empty shopping cart while singing old girl group songs and pantomiming "fellatio" on a long black rubber tube. Up and down, her plump lips traced the length of the tube, her wild tongue shot out lyrics, and her wide hips swung in alarm. Overhead, the only art on the walls hung in a massive frame: a golden-maned lion entering a brawny man who lay prone on the grass. The man's haunches were raised, lips open, mustache wet. His eyes turned toward the ground, but the lion offered the painter a tender look and not one man who saw it didn't sigh. The Lion's Den, the place was called.

"Now every den mother must feed her pride," Miss Teary landed the punch line, after belting out a tough-knuckled song called "The Hunter Gets Captured by the Game."

Miss Carriage rolled her eyes, muttered "suffering fools," and darted for the bar.

The men, and they were all men with ribbed tanks and roper boots, knew the words to all the songs. They waved colored hankies in the air and passed around a bottle of poppers with a screw-top missing. Everyone put a nostril to it; some put two. Round and round the bottle went, and with each huff, I slipped out of myself and the spirits slipped inside. The scent of solvent rose out of the bottle in a vapor that burned away memory. Where you were, the calendar year, the state capitol, the church of your parents, right from wrong, the location of your feet, your own first name, all went like a match in a quick flame.

More memory on fire: the painted face of the angel in the poster. That beauty spot. The brush of rouge.

In a flash, the vapor vanished every thought and magnified every sensation. The furry prickle under your finger nails, the shimmering floaters orbiting your eyes, the loud odor of underwear nearby, all beat with the throttle of the rising floor and the surging heat of the air in your chest. The vapor lifted men off the floor and spun them on their heels, lifted the bar and spun it like a careening carousel. Sounds popped, blood rushed, and for the expanse of a twelve-inch house remix, amyl nitrite lifted every queen out of mourning and made every man into a mindless beast.

With another huff, my chest started to spasm again, and my eyes went black. When they opened, Miss Carriage was nowhere near. I was in a back room of the bar, with the synthesizers muffled and the lights out. My lashes grew heavy and long like feathers and my hands went limp at my sides. My fingers disappeared altogether. My feet kept folding under, while my lungs swelled until I thought they might burst. A few times, I raised my voice but no words fell out, just a gasping sound. My uproar attracted a lion, not the one in the frame but Leon, the long-haired barrel-chested bar owner, who dangled an ornate strand of Mardi Gras beads before me, the old kind made of milky glass.

"Let me have a taste," Leon purred into my ear. When I shook my head "no," he dropped his belt and wrapped the beads around my neck.

"My bar," he said, biting my ear.

"My rules," he said, biting my nipple.

Then he shoved a hankie in my mouth and shoved my face to the floor. Behind me, he dropped his belt, and the sound of a zipper ripped the air. His legs doubled under mine; his hands raced over me. The whole time, he groaned as if someone had him in a headlock. He made choking sounds as if someone had a pair of hands at his throat. He mumbled a smear of French words and chewed at my hair while his whole body trembled and shook. Before he finished, he hacked off a lock with a pocket knife then bared his teeth.

"A perfect little fairy bird," he said.

He squeezed his hand like a gun and put the barrel in my mouth. "And, *mon 'ti cher*, I do love a blackbird gumbo."

Then he threw down the beads. "Fair trade," he said.

Maybe I was only seventeen, but Miss Carriage had taught me the price of trade, and I knew he had yet to pay.

THE NEXT NIGHT, BACK in Lafayette, I snuck into a bar tucked behind a cinder block wall in the back of a nearly abandoned shopping mall. A vinyl store called Raccoon Records had the only open doors by day, and by night the Goth-boy clerk spun dark wave tunes at the bar, the kind no drag queen sang. The electronic beat got the men thrusting their legs in and out on the floor. All around, there were mirrors but the fog kept blocking out the faces so that each dancer was just a pair of legs in the dance or a pair of arms in the air. In and out, they strutted and preened like cranes along the gulf daring each other to take flight first. FANTASY II IN EXILE, the sign over the bar said.

"What happened to Fantasy I?" I asked the Goth-boy DJ before he went down on a longneck and threw the bottle back with nothing but his teeth. A black cross dangled from his ear as if moved by a tremor in the air.

"It got found," a tall guy in spiky hair and white face powder said. There was a silver lightning bolt near his eye and rhinestones where his brows should be. He parted his blue lips. "And any fantasy found is a fantasy killed."

Then he marked the air with a snap and turned back into the fog.

Later that night in his garage apartment, Treats teared up over the lost angel. He was a cousin, distant, but a cousin. Just a boy. Once, he'd taken the stage at Fantasy II draped in nothing but a French flag singing a song by a petite woman known as the Little Sparrow. The queens sneered at his snarky rendition of "La Vie en Rose" and at the safety pin in his ear, but Treats applauded with abandon and dubbed his little cousin a punk diva. He also nursed his cousin through his first STD, a round of syphilis.

"War wounds," Treats called it then, "think of it as Purple Hearts, Toot. You're practically a hero."

Afterward, Treats had meant to stitch up a pink camouflage dress but never got around to it. He swore he had swatches somewhere and towered before the open chest in his studio, pulling out combat boots, tartan kilts, graphic tees, black boas, books on the Beats, and a poster for a show by a factory of artists in New York.

"Nothing," Treats turned to me. "Not a single swatch. Nothing left, sweetie."

The thought seemed to weigh his face down. His hands pulled at the skin and the white powder rubbed off in streaks, making his look redden. His green eyes flared but not at me. He stared over my head and went silent before opening a hinged kit of trays filled with brushes, wands, tubes, and scissors, all ordered in alert rows. They looked like weapons for doll-sized vigilantes. Yet with the powder gone, there was no vengeance in Treats' face. He was younger than Miss Carriage by a decade but already seemed more bowed. Out of the bar, his spiky hair and studded gear became more costume than uniform. With a battery of sponges, his skin darkened into Sabine brown, the burnished color of Cajuns who lived deep back in the bayous. His eyes dimmed too as he flourished a hand, like a magician, over his face.

"It's not drag," he said, "but war paint. Life, that's the real drag."

Then he tossed a boa my way and shimmied out of his chair before popping a pill into his mouth.

"And that's why the gods gave us speed," he said.

The thought put a light back in his eyes, as he swore that *one* hadn't lived until *one* had been to a party on the Mississippi and that's exactly where he'd take me next week. "The Cockfish," he declared, "will make you a man. Or a girl. Your choice, really."

Legend had it, Treats supplied the amber bottles, the white lines, the black beauties, and hormone injections from across the border to half the queens in the state capitol. So I figured Miss Carriage would ride shotgun for another trip over the two bridges to Baton Rouge. The Cockfish was a floating party—"a moveable feast!" as Miss Carriage put it—staged on a former naval ship. When we crossed the plank, I spotted Treats on board, already scouting for business.

"What a lark!" he trilled in the air with an exaggerated smile, as if to convince himself. "What a rush!"

His eyes shut for a long moment before opening again with a piercing look. When he caught sight of Miss Carriage, he genuflected then rose into the towering figure of a royal purveyor, though one with blue lips and a lightning bolt at his eye. He put a hand to his heart and boasted of selling only sunny drugs, "the kind that push your face to the sky, sweetie. Who wants to fall into a crack?"

As he made his pitch, his eyes flitted about in search of a customer in need.

Miss Carriage squeezed my hand. Tonight, she was *in need* but "lacked funds," as she put it. And she was most definitely *she*, in a white wedding gown with a biker belt cinched at her wasp waist and a blonde crown of a wig. She was fighting off a mood, and I didn't need to ask why. The cops hadn't even opened a case on the angel boy yet. No one knew who did it. No suspect in sight. And the motive? They chalked it up to panic defense, especially since the body was found a few hundred yards from a cruise bar.

"Panic," Miss Carriage said, "is an offense *not* a defense. I ask you: how does a dead boy get accused of his own murder?"

Her shoulders shook, and I squeezed her hand back.

"Now," she said, pursing her lips, "time to hunt for a patron. Some flush gent to fund my party favors and put a twirl in this girl."

Then she gave Treats a knowing look and studied his duffel bag. In the background, the lyrics to a song about a sex dwarf spun round and round. Treats closed his eyes then plunged a hand into the bag.

"Listen," he said in a near whisper, "we can't dwell in the dark forever."

His back straightened out of its bow.

"And Lord knows, the best drugs can shake everything into the light."

He placed a white pill in Miss Carriage's palm.

"Ecstasy. The name says it all."

The look on Miss Carriage's face brightened for once, her lips spreading into a wide grin. She almost never showed her teeth, everyone knew. Though she told anyone with ears about the bashing that left her with dentures, she'd learned to smile through tight lips and to talk with more tongue than teeth. Even in Baton Rouge, other queens knew her story, knew how she breathed fire in a bar raid once and led the march to a parish prison to demand the release of an inmate with AIDS. Miss Carriage rarely let go, rarely stopped fighting, so her grin lit up Treats' face too. He grinned right back, his teeth flashing in the strobe lights. And when Miss Carriage offered an I.O.U. Treats refused it with a finger snap.

"Legends twirl for free," he said.

Mostly, Treats operated on a bartering model, with all forms of payment accepted, including finger snaps and party invites, and no line of credit—or favor—denied.

Not the case with The Lion's Den owner, who sold crystal and crank to the rest of the queens in Baton Rouge, the ones who twitched to industrial beats. For that, they rushed to his side and clung to his sleeve.

"Leon has a horde of fans," Treats allowed, "a whole legion."

Yet he whispered doubts about the bar owner and his shady business practices. No one knew where he got his money, for one. And instead of credit, Leon took score. He also took twinks and turned them into trade, Treats warned, looking at Miss Carriage but aiming the warning my way. I pretended not to hear, so Miss Carriage carved an exclamation mark in the air before my eyes.

"Lions and tigers and bears, they're all here and all ready to pounce, so hold onto your basket," she stared me down.

After chaperoning me into an R-rated movie the night before, a movie featuring a dance called the Time Warp and people shouting lines at the screen, Miss Carriage declared me her ward, especially at a party where not everyone "ate from the same mushroom and drank from the same tea."

Yet it didn't take long until Miss Carriage left me for the bar. She knocked back two gold shots in a row then set her eyes to "cruise control." In the middle of the old battleship, a burly guy in a black funeral gown thrashed about to the sound of a drum machine with a stuffed dove wired to his wrist. Behind him, a sign said No Disco! but with a K added in pink lipstick.

"Clever," Miss Carriage said in a rare moment of approval before joining the dance. "After all, I like a good double-entendre."

The sleeves of her gown were capped in white feathers. She raised them to testify to the beat and turned her eyes skyward while I went in search of collecting my pay from a long-haired beast.

Down in the bowels, I passed the nun and priest from the "Bohemian Rhapsody" number, only now the nun had grown a beard and the priest had grown breasts. The priest asked me to open my mouth, then he placed a tab on my tongue. When I asked what, he told me to embrace the mystery. I pushed aside Miss Carriage's warning about clerics and swallowed.

An hour later, the angel boy appeared before my eyes in several places at once: in the parking lot with a shoe missing, a sleeve torn, and an elaborate strand of beads around his neck; in the back of somebody's car with his face shoved to the fogged-over window and a set of claw marks overhead; in the middle of the dance floor frozen while everyone else did the Time Warp. My head flared into a full bonfire now, with memories false and true rising in spires all around. My eyes watered, my throat tightened, and my ribs throbbed me into a spasm. In the fever of my vision, every time a light flashed, the world began anew. The boy's face flashed too, with the beauty spot opening like a small flower on his cheek. I wanted to cry out his name but kept stammering my lips.

Then, when the flashing stopped and the light went steady, I saw it: a set of dentures on the floor in the hall outside the boiler room. They were dim yellow but perfectly formed, like they were made for a singer to open before a microphone. Only there were no sounds coming from the hall or the boiler room, just a rumbling overhead. In a near stupor, I started knocking on every cabin door, busting up more than one coupling, driven with burning nostrils and a flame quickening in my head. I bolted back up to the deck and pushed my way through the crowd looking for a trail of white feathers. Yet there was no sign of Miss Carriage anywhere, not a single plume.

Until I heard an odd but familiar sound coming from the galley. A kind of choking and an ugly smear of French words. When I threw open the door, Leon had Miss Carriage on her back and a billystick in his hand. He'd come dressed as a cop, complete with a shiny badge. Miss Carriage was handcuffed, and her wig was knocked off. A bruise shone on her neck, and a line of blood trailed from her ear. She stared at me with fixed eyes, and I stared back with a shaking head. In the haze of the moment, the Lion ran past me toward the door. Without her teeth, Miss Carriage kept her lips tight. My own tongue stuttered and failed to get out a word. Yet a sharp sound ripped right from my throat, like a war cry.

For a moment, the dance music halted, and feathers hung in the air. Doors flew open, all ears turned to the galley, and out of nowhere Miss Teary de la Place burst into the room. When she caught sight of Miss Carriage, her shriek echoed mine. Her chest rose, her wig shook, and she yelled "LEON!" long and loud as a siren wailing over the whole ship.

In a rush, a flock of queens raced across the deck to answer Miss Teary's call. They soon figured out the whole story and resolved to find the beast who'd struck Miss Carriage. The music started up again, and the leather daddies, cowboys, and jocks turned back to dancing, but the queens turned to riot. They hurled empty rocks glasses, loaded beer cans, and extra large high heels across the deck. They threw glass vials and amber bottles. They shot pint glasses and shakers into the air, and the wind picked it all up and slammed it against the bow with a great crashing sound. Treats pumped a fist and led the hunt for Leon past the bridge and down the gangway. The sky filled with glitter dust and silky down and barbed bits of feather, and the floor covered over with a silvery powder. Heads turned port and starboard and port again for any sign of the long-haired bar owner. Suddenly, Treats let out a screeching sound and grazed Leon with the sharp edge of a broken bottle, just before he leapt onto the plank.

"Drown the Lion!" Treats shouted to the air.

With a clap of thunder, he went racing down the bouncing strip of lumber, and I ran in his hot footsteps. The acid surged in my head, and the cones of light on the water trembled like underwater speakers pumping heavy voltage. A shock of motion agitated the surface, radiating like a strobe, and the current cast eyes everywhere, as the river filled with floating faces. Treats threw his hands up and streaks of powder ran down his cheeks. My chest throbbed and vision wavered. Leon had jumped; he might've been anywhere. He might've pulled himself onto another ship and disappeared into the night, like the killer who battered the angel boy. We'd never know the killer's name, never know where he lurked, and we'd never know justice. Red dots pulsed before my eyes and gray smoke hung overhead. Even if we could rid Leon of his mane, rid the scene of Leon, we'd lived in his den without ever catching his scent. Was it too familiar? Too close to our own? Heat rose up like vapor, as the muddy Mississippi swallowed each cone of light. The whole scene went dark, and my ears echoed with vanishing beats, until a curtain of silence dropped overhead.

Treats turned on his heels, and I turned around too. My chest throbbed again, louder and louder, yet when I looked back, I saw that the water wasn't filled with floating faces. There was merely one face, blurry and dim, in the distance. Next I saw a golden flash, a mane of hair, and heard a far-off gasp for air. My tongue stammered, and my mouth stuck on one odd sound. But my lips finally let fly a whole word, steady and clear: "Vengeance!" It was only one word, still it brought back Miss Carriage's vow. As the smoke cleared, I shot a finger straight at Leon's dim figure in the water, and every pair of eyes looked dead ahead. Treats jumped, I jumped, and a dozen others jumped overboard, all of us flapping madly to stay afloat. The Lion was a hundred strokes away, swimming like a hunted catfish, but he faced only the opposite bank. He couldn't see what we saw: a crest of waves parting in our path, light beaming from our eyes. He couldn't hear what we heard: a chorus soaring at our back, a song beating in our ear. No, he couldn't escape us now. Long legs, long necks, sharp beaks, we were a siege of cranes. Red crowns, white napes, we were ready to trouble the water and charge the air. Together, we were ready to take wing.

12.

MAKEUP

In our prom picture, my date was the pretty one, not me. With raven hair, ivory skin and an angular face, she looked designed for the banner: FOREVER HOLLYWOOD. She fit the role of Prom Date like an ace actress. Yet I didn't fit and knew it. I'd only been cast in the role as a last minute stand-in when another guy bowed out and Jazz, who'd arranged a double date with two sisters, called my number.

Jazz counted on me for essays, exams, and an extra arm for anything he didn't care to carry: textbooks, duffel bags, even the bulky keys to his truck.

"Can't kill the silhouette," he said, while assessing himself in the mirror or in the faces of girls passing in the hall.

His name was J.S. but the whole campus called him Jazz for his flashy out-of-town style. He'd moved all the way from Dallas and brought satin jackets and gelled hair to campus. On him, a turned-up collar, blond streaks, and a pierced ear looked more guy than girl. Even his no-sock shoes hit the ground with certain force. Neither a jock nor a brain, a nerd nor a geek, he made his way through the halls with slick hair and slick poses and seemed to know how to do nothing better than anyone else. One leg propped against a post, one foot kicked into the air. One arm wrapped around the back of a desk, one hand raked through his hair. Jazz had a half-there half-gone look in his eyes that allowed him to slip through the rope of high school rules. Only a jock should've asked the head cheerleader on a date, but no one was shocked when Jazz held up a sign with the question—right in front of the quarterback and right in the middle of class—or when she said yes.

Her younger sister, Delta, was part of the deal, and now I carried something else for Jazz: an ill-fitting tux. The borrowed suit was meant for a guy with football shoulders and soccer legs. I cinched the waist with a skinny belt and pulled the loose fabric into a new seam with a zigzag of safety pins. Then I double-knotted a tie and pushed up the sleeves. If you squinted from across a very dark room, you might've imagined you saw a guy in a suit. Yet in the light, the suit still billowed and was so misshapen that I looked like a popsicle melting in the sun, with the stick ready to snap out of its molded form. When she opened the screen door, Delta pursed her lips but said nothing. Maybe she saw the baggy tux as another odd piece in a disarrayed puzzle. Or maybe she saw past me to the prom, where she'd be the only freshman, and who cared how she got there?

What Delta saw, at least at first, worried me less than Jazz. What did he see—or not see? Was I his secret, so out in the open no one would notice? When Jazz first took me as his sidekick, with my bangled wrists and flame-red hair, the kids and teachers chalked it up to another of his eccentricities. Maybe his Roman nose, his square jaw, and his steady eye cast him as more young man than teenage boy, and maybe that role placed a permit in his hands. A young man was independent. A young man was allowed certain risks. He could stand next to a teenage boy, especially a teenage fairy boy, and his stance would look even tougher. Beside him, I must've looked submissive as a pillow or a punching bag. Jazz never swung a joke at me, though, and never hit me with a name. Instead, he let me shadow his silhouette and walk the halls by his side.

Yet at prom, it was the head cheerleader, not me, by his side. It was her sister, a girl four years younger, next to me. Someone might shout a name, my name. Someone might point at the Jenny Woman in the tux, the sissy in the suit. The air might explode in stormy laughter, ridicule raining down like a turned-over bucket of confetti, scorn flashing from bared teeth.

Every party began with a sacrifice, I knew, and ended with a confession. It was one thing to show my feathers at school by day, to dangle charms and beads. It was another thing to tuck my wings and hide my colors, to pass as a guy on a date with a girl, or to pass as a normal guy at all. Who'd cuff my hands first? Who'd call my bluff? Who'd muffle my mouth and deliver my penance?

By senior year, I had much to confess but few secrets left. The lock had long blown off my cover. Even so, an empty chest doesn't mean fear has left the room. In the schoolhouse of the disco, I'd learned courage in a gay bar with gay men, but courage away is not courage at home. Also: virtue in one world is vice in another. And at a Catholic high school, castigation follows vice every time, no matter how false or unfair the charge. Every week, the kneeler in the church confessional groaned while I opened my mouth to let loose a new story. Every week, the priest leaned closer to the screen, listening to my voice rise higher, the lower the act, the more twisted the end.

What everyone knew: no crayoned valentine, no sweetheart carnation, no origamied love note, no aching heart mixtape had ever passed between a girl's hands and mine. What everyone knew: instead, a boy's hands had passed over my head and pushed me to my knees, a boy's hands had pulled my pants to the ground. What everyone knew: it happened more than once, with more than one boy, then it happened with a man, an older man, a teacher and even a priest. What everyone knew: I was fallen, I was graceless, I was doomed, I was one lost sheep.

What no one knew: I liked it that way. I wanted it that way.

What I knew: I was not the only one.

When we walked through the prom door, though, what everyone saw was Jazz and the cheerleader, their grins wide and bright and easy. Delta and I slipped in behind them, and the band blasted a whistle while a singer belted, "You dropped a bomb on me!" Jazz cast a look my way: no bucket turned over my head, no confetti rained down. Maybe he was right.

"Gotta fake it to make it," he'd told me before meeting the girls.

Prom was fairy tale night, after all, with a grand theme, swollen-faced characters, dazzling old-world costumes, and fantastic settings. Even so, no one ever mistook the dwarf for a giant or the elf for a prince. And no one, I was sure, mistook me for a romantic lead.

Especially not Delta. In the blinking lights of the room, I could see her face in close-up. Makeup brought her features into focus: two dramatic streaks of blush, copper lips, smoky shadow, and cat eyes drawn with heavy liner. She wore a serious world-weary expression, like a debutante already tired of the balls and the boys and the boorish talk. If she were in a film, she'd play the ingénue turned sophisticate—or vamp—before the final act. She even smoked the clove cigarette Jazz passed around with more style than any of us, her cheeks flush as petals and her eyes blazing with secret knowledge.

The four of us found a table and sat, but not for long. Jazz kept cracking his knuckles and knocking his knee under the table, and Delta's sister kept craning her head around the room. Maybe she hadn't noticed Jazz wasn't much of a talker. With all his slick poses and slick looks, no one seemed to catch on that he said very little. Yet I'd learned that he asked more questions than he answered. Even when we were alone in his pick-up, he mostly just nodded his head to whatever I said, in a dreamy indeterminate way, not yes or no but something in the middle. So to cut the silence at the prom table, I told stories about weird midnight movies or New Wave bands with space age gear and futuristic looks, my hands rising in one wild arc after another. Delta smiled in a lopsided way. Yet Jazz stared at me as if there was a question mark flashing on my face, and his date stared at the dance floor as if it was a planet spinning in outer space.

Suddenly, Jazz bolted up from the table and seized the cheerleader's hand. The two of them cut right through the crowd with a series of quick-fire moves until she pretended to faint in his arms and he pretended to revive her with a long wet kiss and a hand on her waist. Then his hand seemed to pull a string that sent her spinning out of and back into his arms in a dizzying whirl. By that point, the other dancers had stopped moving, and the band turned their brass instruments to the couple of the moment.

When a glove grabbed my hand, I startled. Then I looked up and saw Delta. Did she expect me to dance? To move like Jazz? When she feigned a yawn and angled her head toward the photo stand, relief lifted me out of my chair. All around the gym, a series of brightly colored facades had been raised, one-dimensional homes from famous movies or TV shows. The people painted in the windows seemed frozen in time but the timeline itself seemed warped with a Victorian mansion sitting next to a California ranch house next to a French Quarter cottage next to a Manhattan penthouse. When she saw me lagging, Delta tugged me forward with her gloved hand. I could feel my popsicle stick body weaving, from the heat, from the champagne, and from the sudden fear of what might happen next.

In the long line leading up to the Hollywood banner and the glittery backdrop, a circle of girls applied and reapplied mascara, eyeliner, and lipstick, raising hand mirrors this way and that, searching each other's faces for approval, sometimes offered, sometimes denied. Whose face could I search? I wondered. Whose head would nod yes or no? But Delta didn't seem to wonder—about my approval or the other girls. Apart from her sister, she grew taller and her neck grew longer while I shrank further into my tux. How long until she beamed her eyes right through mine? How long until I disappeared altogether?

With that gray cloud of worry overhead, the camera snapped its own hot eye at Delta and me. I stood dazed before Jazz nudged me with the tip of his shoe to move out of view. Arm in arm, he and the cheerleader both flashed a brilliant illustrated magazine smile, a smile that shone with long walks and long plans, with a wide lawn and high ceilings and a pair of trophy-winning kids. The photographer clapped his hands in front of his face and made a splashing sound with his mouth. Maybe Jazz didn't say much, but he knew how to impress. Suddenly, other guys clutched their dates tighter and moved in closer for the camera.

Next, the four of us plodded back to the round table where even our glittery centerpiece wilted from the heat. The glue ran in rivulets, and the glitter dotted the table in cloudbursts. Though a giant fan hummed in a corner, the heat in the gym was nearly visible, with a kind of oily vapor. Delta was panting a bit and her sister's forehead was glistening when I caught Jazz's eye. He stared me down, as if I was about to reveal a secret no one, not even he, had guessed. Then he slammed a flat palm down on the edge of the table.

"Are you ready, boy?" he asked.

Together, we had arrived at the prom in a rented white limo, but now we had to leave in Jazz's stretch-cab truck, since the cheerleader had lost her pink champagne and most of her crawfish dinner on the limo floor.

"Ready, boy?" Jazz shouted again over the frantic rush of a song about a used condom and a fast car. His face winked. The fizz of dying champagne filled my ears. The room buzzed, the music blurred, and all the lights went fire red. When I looked at Delta and saw her makeup melting, I took it as a sign.

"Yeah," I blurted, "Ready."

Outside, Delta tugged the ends of her black corset gown into the cab then I clambered in beside her. Jazz somehow threw the truck into first, second, and third gear while holding onto the steering wheel and the cheerleader's hand at the same time. The revved-up truck grew fins and flares and finally spoiler wings as he sped through flashing yellow lights, raced through an abandoned parking lot and over a small ditch before bringing the truck like a jet to a jerking halt. The high beam pointed toward the dark and gated entrance of the park. Jazz shut off the ignition and cut off the lights.

"Guess we're gonna sit here a while," he said, running a hand along the dashboard down to the cheerleader's thigh. When I didn't answer, he added, "Her and me."

Though dazed, I heard the prompt, stepped out of the truck, then stumbled around the other side to give Delta a trembling hand. Without saying a word to each other, she and I walked foot by foot to a mossy bench near a pond. From our wood-slat seat, we watched the windows of the truck cover with steam. We watched geese quarrel and make up on the algae-smothered pond. We watched billowing clouds form shapes overhead then part in two. There seemed to be a script in view, and I thought I could read the lines well enough. I opened my mouth to speak before a goose honked and Delta burst out laughing.

"You're beautiful," I said, not exactly sure if that was the word. It sounded rehearsed and phony, and she called me on it.

"Don't you mean handsome?"

My face pulled into a puzzle.

"Heaven knows I'm no flower. At least, that's not what I wanna be. Flowers are beautiful, sure, but then they lose their heads and fall."

I couldn't help it: I laughed then slapped my hand on my mouth. Delta laughed too, not in delicate ribbons but in a long great sheet of sound. Then her face grew stern.

"And don't call me pretty either," she said. "My sister is pretty. Pretty girls lead cheers and study boys. Can you think of anything duller than that?"

Delta laughed again, looking dead at me. On the bench, she was eye-level again, no longer taller, and when she pulled her hair back, I could see her flat ears and an ankh tattoo hidden under her sleeve.

"Okay, you're handsome," I said. "And too smart for a freshman."

She removed a glove and rapped my hand once with the tips of her fingers.

"I only see what I see and know what I know."

Her eyes narrowed and her brow furrowed. *Was that my cue?* I worried. I thought I was following the lines but fell into confusion. *Should I kiss her? Was that what she wanted?* No doubt, she knew who I was, what I was, but did she still want a kiss?

When I nudged closer to her side of the bench and adjusted my arm so that it slid behind her waist, her face relaxed into a shimmering glow and her lips parted a bit.

The bench began to sweat, not from bayou heat but from a chilly fever that stole over me. Mist raced across the grass and rushed up my leg. Clouds gathered into a hovering gray mass, blotting out the moon. Each breath seemed shorter, colder. The air closed in tighter and my hands shook. Then in a mad flash, I shut my eyes and brought my lips in a rush to Delta's neck. My tongue stung from the amber of her perfume. Almost drunk, my head grew dizzy and though Delta's mouth was moving, I couldn't make out what she was saying. Wild now in my effort to perform, my hand squeezed hard on her breast, as if I might draw sustenance from it. She shrieked out a laugh—I could hear that—then covered my face with hers. She opened her mouth, and her tongue slid between my lips and across my tongue. I sat still and went stiff, feeling the weight of her tongue on mine. Like fur on rubber. Like velvet on eel. When she pulled her face back, my hand still held the bodice of her dress, and one breast popped out. The white globe and bright blue veins filled my eyes in an extreme close-up. Now I was ready to confess everything: every extended trip to the locker room, every hand down my pants, every boy in my mouth, every bit she already knew. Then all she didn't know: every time Jazz called me up at night, every time he drove me out to a field and laid me on the leather seat of his cab, every time he blew a kiss out the window. My mouth hung open, the words had all rushed out. Next a heaving sound surrounded me, like a great chest exploding. The sound rippled into a scream, and my hands rose to my ears before they began slapping my face. Delta looked at me in horror, I thought, as if I might burst through my shoes to reveal cloven hooves. Yet when she spoke, her voice sounded soothing like the all-knowing debutante in a black-and-white movie. The boy she dated thought he'd fooled her into thinking he was another guy, an up-and-coming young man. But she was never fooled. Near the end as he faced doom, she cradled the moody boy and her eyes glowed like violet embers. "Tell Mama," she said to the top of his head, "Tell Mama all."

For a moment, Delta let me rest my head on her shoulders while my heaving settled into a quiet sob. But soon the quiet was broken by a loud voice.

"Ready?" Jazz shouted across the pond. "Ready, boy?"

The truck headlights beamed at us. Delta lifted the curtain of her bodice and tucked the white globe into place.

"Ready, punk!" she hollered back at the truck for me.

We locked eyes. It was a lie, the kind told in movies with an ending and credits and people walking out in a daze. I wasn't ready at all. When Delta stood, she pulled out a compact mirror and a powdered brush to pat my face dry.

"There," she said in a whisper. "There you are."

Back in the truck, I looked closely at Jazz's date for the first time. Delta was right: she was pretty. Sapphire eyes, golden hair, ruby lips. And a carnation-pink dress. Yet her face looked angry, like a girl who figured there'd be more to prom than a bumpy ride to a park in a pick-up. Her face turned away from Jazz toward the window, and for a long time she stared into the night and the passing lights. Jazz said nothing, as usual, but his nothing crackled in the air and turned his knuckles white on the steering wheel. His hands gripped tighter and tighter. Both hands, I noticed. He didn't hold the cheerleader's hand and only moved his arms when he had to shift gears. Under a stoplight, his knee shifted, looking for the right position. Then Delta's sister angled her head back to whisper.

"Birds of a feather," she said.

When Delta kept her lips pursed, her sister tried again.

"Two of a kind," she said, louder and looking now at me.

Jazz's heart beat so fast I could hear it. Delta must've heard it too. She cleared her throat as if she was about to sing, but instead she started humming. It was a funny sound strung together with little hiccups of laughter. Yet she wasn't laughing at Jazz or me, I knew.

"And what kind of bird are you?" she asked her sister. "Canary or crow?"

Then she continued humming, and Jazz threw the truck back into gear. His hands relaxed on the wheel, and his eyes caught mine in the rear view mirror. The cheerleader turned her head and pressed her face to the window, but Delta kept humming and humming. Jazz began humming too, lower and louder than Delta, and I joined along, the three of us humming and hiccupping and howling our way into the wide open night, into the wild and fantastic unknown.

13.

TWO-HEADED BOY

The blood was drawn into vials by a plasma center on campus, where I went under the needle twice a week. The vials looked like glass bullets, and the blood looked bright at first, almost vermilion, then darkened to cardinal. Yet all I could see was green: cash flowing for the booze and blotters that fueled my first year of college. The donor center paid for each draft of plasma with easy money. The exchange rate ran to my favor until the day I approached the front desk and an orderly gave me a hard stare then gripped my folder with alarm. My black leggings, velvet jacket, and silver rosary glowed in his eyes as if in ultraviolet light, as if radioactive. Between us, a four-letter word sparked like static, my blood stopped, and the air went dead.

"No doubt about it," the orderly said through tight lips as he walked me to a windowless room at the back of the clinic, "AIDS." He'd run a second test, but it'd take a month and he'd never seen a false positive. Never. Anyway, I had the symptoms, didn't I?

"Where there's smoke..." he started then stopped, one freckled hand covering his mouth. Then he waved at the air and counted the symptoms on his fingers, like a Sunday school teacher listing the Ten Plagues of Egypt.

Fatigue, fever, swollen glands. Dry cough, skin rash, sudden weight loss. Night sweats, nausea, phantom sensations in the feet and hands. I showed every sign of affliction.

What's more, I *was* queer, wasn't I?

The orderly reminded me of my perjury in signing the official weekly donation form. In Louisiana, gay blood was as outlaw as absinthe and presumed just as toxic. Only the green fairy conducted a plague of one, while the lavender virus ushered gay men by the dozens then by the hundreds and thousands out of classrooms, theaters, and studios, out of bars, bathhouses, and discos. I'd lied, it was true, for the money, for the drugs. There was no more relief in the confession than in dropping a letter in a casket. No one would answer it, no one would even hear it fall. Yet at least the clinic wouldn't press charges. After all, as the orderly put it, I already had the death sentence.

"Six months," he said while staring into the folder. "Time to make some plans."

But any plans had long been set in place. After a failed clip of my lisping tongue by a surgeon, a failed cure of my swishing walk by a psychiatrist, and a failed conversion of my wandering eye by a priest, my mother foresaw the diagnosis. No trophy, ribbon, or medal, no string of A's, tower of awards, or stack of university letters could redeem a degenerate son. She'd warned me I'd be afflicted, warned me of the abomination of mortal sin, of eyes going blind and body parts falling off.

Now that her early prediction was confirmed, she banned me from home. Over the phone, she prophesied my end: stripped to the bone, stripped of every muscle, stripped of all pride. I could nearly see her, testifying to the ceiling with her free hand, appealing to the congregation of furniture to witness the shame of her motherhood. No doubt, even the pale cream covering her cheeks flashed red, and her hair sprang out of its straight wedge into a coil of disgrace. In her voice, I could hear the mask of righteous anger, but then I also could hear the naked sorrow of a woman staring at her son's empty bedroom like an unoccupied bassinet. My whole head fit in her hands once, both my feet fit against her lips. Yet I grew like a monster to tower over her, to outrun her. I fled home to sleep with other monsters, other two-headed men, and now the virus was God's thunderbolt of judgment. Man lying with man was as grievous a sin as infidelity or incest in the eyes of the Lord. Man lying with man was as abhorrent as man lying with beast.

"Blood shall be upon the sinner," she said, with a firm click of her tongue. "Forget plans. Time to make penance."

Instead, I made haste. And a trip to the mall. There, I picked up a black tuxedo shirt, a high collar trench coat, and a crucifix earring. I was only nineteen, but I knew how to dress for a funeral, especially one where I'd be the guest of honor. And I knew how to deliver a valediction from a stage.

When I dared to make plans of my own, they were mapped out in my dorm room before bed. I'd smuggle onboard a plane to Paris, where I'd throw my skinny body down on grave after grave in Père Lachaise cemetery. I'd lie in a glass coffin in the middle of the Vatican, my corpse incorruptible. I'd emerge one night on a stage in New York with flowers in my back pocket singing a song I'd written only hours before. I'd chew every book in the library by day and swallow every shot in the bar by night. I'd marry the DJ, the doorman, the professor. It would all happen fast in flash after flash and turn after turn. Then I'd wake to a set of shadow eyes on the sheets and a silhouette of sweat.

Soon, the follow-up test would punctuate my sentence, but I had no patience and wanted to see the end. If I dosed before the diagnosis, then I double-dosed now. If I set the weekend on fire before, now I burned each day. Vials of my blood sat in a fluorescent clinic, awaiting analysis, but I danced under strobe lights, awaiting only the next high. Black beauties, white crosses, angel dust, the drugs were not just holy medicine but a sacred arsenal. Little bullets to kill the time. Little arrows to quell the mind. My mother couldn't be right. The orderly couldn't be wrong. And lying with men couldn't be both.

"God don't like selfish," my mother had said about homo sex.

But she was wrong, wasn't she? Almost always, I had slipped out of myself during sex, had shed my skin, shaken off my body. There was no self left, no getting and no giving either. No grace and no curse. There was only a hum, a kind of music two men made. The jagged clash of a punk song, the velvet push of a ballad. Sex with older men, with a den of priests, teachers, and jocks. Sex in public places, in a den of tents, showers, and locker rooms. Sex on bunk beds, in the hush of confessionals and sugar cane fields. No, I tried to convince myself. Sex with other men hadn't shown me a mirror but a diamond, a turntable, and a groove. The exit music from home.

Yet the exit carried a toll. And at party after party, disco after disco, I paid until my credit ran out.

At the climax of one house party, nearly a month after my diagnosis, club kids filled the living room with neon platform shoes, candy-colored vinyl, and towering hats. A leggy drag queen in a black lace bustier and white pearls longer than my rosary rolled her eyes, declared she was "over the rainbow, girl" then waved me into a bedroom with a flickering red bulb and a hovering cloud of incense. There, I forgot about home, every prediction and prophecy, forgot about college, every essay and exam. Forgot the name of the host, the name of the queen shaking a bottle in my hand, the name of the day. I forgot numbers too. How many hands on the clock, how many fingers in the air, how many pills. Only one thought pulsed: *How long is now?* Six months, the orderly had said. No doubt about it, AIDS. In less than a week, the proof would arrive. I chased the thought with black beauties and chased the beauties with blue devils and chased myself into a speedball. With the rush of speed and the drag of downers, I dropped to the floor in a fit of convulsions. My eyes froze open and the party ran in a reverse loop with cue marks as the queen split, the club kids bailed, and two ambulances and a fire truck beamed red light into the house. Men in uniform surrounded me when I heard the party host speak in a clipped voice.

"No, officer, I haven't the faintest idea what happened," he said over my head, as my chest wracked in spasms on the floor. "We were just sitting here chatting away when he rolled over and started choking on his tongue."

In the hollow of my ears, it sounded like the description of a glass shaken off the counter by a mysterious vibration. A small loss of no real concern. Until the shattering sound rang into an endless echo, a deafening, deadening siren tearing right through the night.

THE NEXT MORNING, I awoke to a voice reading from the final passage of a story. The writer told of an aging professor seated on a beach, hair painted black, cheeks dusted with carmine, and lips rouged into the dark red of strawberries. The very picture of a corpse. Yet the old man's alert eyes traveled the shoreline in search of a young boy, a tourist who flitted in and out of view, with a glowing head of hair. He called out the boy's name in a whisper as his makeup melted in the killing heat of the sun. A plague had driven nearly everyone else off the beach. A camera tripod stood abandoned, umbrellas and huts vacant, no attendant in sight. Behind the professor, the walls of the town were washed white with a pungent disinfectant. Yet the boy stood oblivious, contrapposto, with the crests of waves at his feet, before another boy tugged him down into the sand. They wrestled with such a fury the professor thought they both might drown until the golden-haired boy rose up, and he rose to meet him, arms outstretched and stiff as a cadaver. The story ended there, with the old man dead, but the voice added a moral: "When you grow up, honey lamb, don't chase little boys or they'll break open your brain and fry it like an egg in the sun."

The laugh that ripped from my lips tore out of the reader's mouth too, and I found myself face to face with Mercy, the reigning queen of the state psych ward, where the ODs, self-harmers, and convulsives were lumped with the lunatics, maniacs, and all but the criminally insane. She'd smuggled the book out of a haphazard hospital library and read it to me like medicine, with passages spooned out and coated in her molasses voice. She liked to add her own twist, she said, because writers always let her down at the end.

"They kill the homo or lock him up in the asylum, so I play Lady Jesus and perform a miracle. Cure, exorcism, resurrection, you name it."

"What about the force of nature?" I asked.

"What about it?" she answered, with a snap of her tongue. "Look at me. I am divine. What do I have to do with nature?"

Then she lifted her hands up in the shape of a square, like a viewfinder on a camera, and pointed the lens at me.

"A bit of a fixer-upper," she declared, "but you'll do fine."

"Do what?" I asked, but she just wagged her finger in the motion of a metronome, waiting for me to follow the beat.

Even seated, I could tell she was tall, basketball player tall. She wore the same prison-gray gown as the rest of the ward but with one side tied into a knot, as if she were at the port of New Orleans drinking daiquiris with a sailor. With paper clips, she had fashioned finger curls and let one long tail of hair rest on her shoulder. Her cheeks flushed light pink, with a perpetual look of astonishment, and her eyes glowed, even with no mascara, liner, or shadow. For all her height, she sat poised as a starlet in a soda shop, legs crossed twice, at the knee and the ankle, making the folding chair look like a bar stool.

"How long have you done drag?" I asked.

"Honey, I don't *do* drag. I am a woman…"

"…born in the wrong body?"

"Born in the wrong century! And what is this obsession with 'do'? You've got your verbs all screwed up, little mister. The verb you want is 'be.' 'Do' for others but 'be' for yourself. Get it?"

When I asked why she'd read the story of the professor to me, she puckered her pink lips, arched her plucked brow, and proclaimed, "Trust! Takes one to know one."

With a wink, she rose out of her chair and strutted out the room, while the book balanced like a feather on her head. And I was left to wonder: what exactly did she know? Had she seen my diagnosis?

Even more: what exactly did my mother know? Had she been right? Had she prophesied my end—alone, with bad blood and a ghostly body?

Over the long weekend, Mercy read half a dozen books to me, sometimes while I dozed, slipping in and out of awareness. The stories mostly were queer, with a hunchback dwarf, a giant woman, a pair of deaf mutes, and a girl whose crutch moved like a third leg. There was an execution, a crucifixion, and more than one star-crossed boy in a three-way love affair. Everyone wound up alone or dead, so Mercy improvised a new ending or transitioned abruptly from the final words of a tragic story to a punch line from *Mad Magazine* or sunny news from *The Hollywood Reporter* about a budding romance amid co-stars.

Once, I stopped Mercy in the middle of an improvised resurrection.

"Just desserts," I said about the doomed man. Thinking: *Selfish*. Thinking: *Degenerate*. Thinking: *Let the homo die.* He'd been a lusty sailor, a druggy thief, an unruly prisoner. A poisonous flower of a man. He'd seduced a cop, a judge, a guard, yet loved only his own slick palm. Wasn't there logic in a story? Live by the sword, die by the sword. Fuck with abandon, die with abandon.

"Nothing sweet in that dessert," Mercy said. "Besides, fuck is not the opposite of death any more than life is the opposite of fuck."

"Is this the lesson?" I asked, cranky from the buzzing lights and flashing machines and flaming voices, cranky from the comedown of a towering disco high. "Is this what I'm here to learn? A riddle? A nursery rhyme? That one and one is not two, that the opposite of lie is not true?"

"In case you haven't noticed, little story killer, you are strapped to a bed, plugged to an IV, and walled off by a curtain. There's no seat on the toilet, no lock on the door, and no sharp object on the desk. Class was dismissed as soon as you opened your mouth and swallowed a fistful of rage."

"OD," I said. "I just OD'd."

"Just?" Mercy asked as she turned toward the door. "As in 'just desserts'?"

This time, I bit my tongue. What did I know? I didn't even know my own blood test. Live, die, fuck, love were odd words that rattled in my mouth. "Trust," Mercy had said. Another word I didn't know.

Every few hours, nurses padded in and out of the room and doctors prodded me with needles. One broad-backed orderly walked spine-straight with a military buzz cut and patent leather shoes. His shoulders, chest, jaw, even his hair, all if it a perfect square, an architect's sketch of a man. He almost never spoke in my direction, except to give a command. Open wide, shut, roll over. Yet I recognized his solid voice, the steady sound of a man who fit his skin. Maybe he drew my blood upon admittance. Maybe he knew the proof of the second test. But he kept his mouth sealed and his eyes on the chart in his hands. When he turned on his heels, a cloud of tobacco and turpentine followed, while a phantom musk surrounded my bed. Did he ever shift his eyes? Did he sway his walk? Did he open his mouth or unzip in the hush of another room?

Down the hall, patients broke the silence when they lined up for bright red gelatin molds. Foam slippers busily shuffled back and forth, and applause boomed and echoed. "Oh Lordy," I could hear Mercy shout every time a pill cup met a pair of praying hands. "Lordy! Lordy! Lordy!"

On Sunday, family filled the lobby with a low buzz and the crinkle of new magazines or goodie bags. But my parents didn't visit, didn't call, and with the gloomy synthesizer of a Goth song in my head, I wondered if I'd ever see the exit sign to Charity. I wondered if my last six months would end on a hospital bed in a psych ward like a fox with his tail caught in a trap.

"Does he sacrifice his tail to live free?" I asked out loud, "Or keep the tail and die whole?"

"Such melodrama," Mercy cautioned, "can only give you heartburn. And trust! No one wants to romance a boy with acid reflux. What you need is…"

"Mercy," I joked.

"Lordy, no," she answered, ignoring the pun with an elaborate wave of her hand. "No one needs mercy. Mercy runs like water in the body; it's always there. All you have to do is swallow, and you can taste mercy. A liar, a cheat, a thief, even a killer has mercy in his mouth, honey lamb. A new story, that's what you need."

The next day, after nightfall, Mercy broke into the nurses' station, slipped my file between her legs, and returned to my room to read what she called the Story of My Life.

"I can already tell you how it ends," I said. "I get AIDS."

"What kind of fiction is that?" She screwed up her face. "That's not a story; it's a sentence. And it's certainly no joke."

"No fiction," I answered, "No joke. Blood test."

Mercy flared her eyes and opened her mouth but said nothing. Her lips shut as she sat back in the chair and stared at her palms, as if trying to remember what she had last held. With a quick-knotted fist, she yanked hard on the tail of hair at her shoulder and bolted to her feet. She stepped close to the bed, stooped over my head then let her mouth open over mine. Instead of rose or violet, she smelled of red berries and camphor. At first, I kept my mouth closed as she puckered her lips and inhaled, but the power in her breath pulled the air out of my chest and my lips finally parted. Then she slipped her tongue past my teeth where it sat like an oversized lozenge. Instead of melting, though, with menthol and hard sugar, it thickened into soft suede then wet leather. The tongue hammered at the roof of my mouth before my own tongue started to hammer and a blue fire burst into my forehead. Suddenly, her breath drew back with such force that her cheeks collapsed and her eyes locked into place and I was sure she was having a seizure until she recoiled her tongue, snapped her body straight, and said, "You got nothing."

"You could tell from a kiss?" I asked.

"You can tell a lot from a kiss, trust! But no." Her tongue made a popping noise, like an egg in a frying pan. "Lordy, no. I read your file. You don't have AIDS. Wanna know the real story?"

For the first time since I'd awakened on the ward, a cough broke out of my mouth. A long, wet cough. While I'd been asleep, my chest had steadied, and the fever had cooled. My skin remained red, and my ribs still showed, but my feet and hands no longer throbbed. Had the plasma center found a false positive? Had AIDS been a phantom in my body?

When the cough died down, Mercy placed the file on my chest. She'd just turned thirty-three, her Jesus year, as she put it. More than a dozen years since she sprang out of her mother's closet at nineteen, same age as me, flashing a rose-colored negligee and a pair of stilettos. She was an adult by then, draft age, voting age, drinking age, but her parents committed Mercy to a ritzy hospital in another parish, where they shot electricity into her brain.

"Ever since," she said, "I get these tremors, and a knot swells up in my throat until I can't breathe and a blue fire burns in my forehead and my tongue hammers against my teeth. The scourge, my family calls it. Collateral damage, I say. They aimed for my light but only rattled the socket. I still glow and, yes, honey lamb, I radiate."

I wanted to ask Mercy about the fire I'd seen in my own forehead but knew better than to interrupt her in the middle of a story. It's like a hurricane, she'd told me. Just when the eye of the tale moves overhead and the winds ease up, that's when you know the climax is coming.

"All that heavy voltage failed to dim my girlish glimmer, so the doctors pumped me with bromides then shocked me out of the coma with insulin while my parents stared at me with no lips and no ears. Their faces bore only a pair of shaded eyes. Always at the end, my father would clap my back hard, as if a pink pellet might shoot right out my mouth and onto the floor, where my mother could pick it up, wrap it in tissue, and hide it in her purse. Like a tube of lipstick she meant to discard. When they split, the purse shut, and I ended up here, a dried-up fruit in a bowl of nuts."

Mercy stared into her palms again while her fingers danced in little spasms.

"You're no fruit," I said. "Fruits are sweet or tart, one or the other. You're both."

She screwed her lips tight, as if I'd call out her birth certificate name.

"And you're not dried-up either."

"No?" Mercy answered. "Then tell me: who hungers for a middle-aged flat-chested giantess? Who visits the bed of a spastic pre-op tranny?"

"The military orderly," I said. It was a guess. But I pictured him pinning down Mercy's hands while he stared at the white walls, the fluorescent lights, the heart monitor until his musk filled the room and he commanded her to swallow.

"If you know about that," Mercy said, "then you know too much." She waved her finger back and forth. "Time for you to go, honey lamb."

"You're an adult. Why don't you sign yourself out? Why don't you leave?"

"It's one thing to leave. It's another to go."

Her hands tugged at the knot in her hospital gown until a notebook page fell out. It was a list, a set of prescriptions for behavior. I knew that list. I'd called it out to Mercy one night, telling her of my parents' search for a gay cure, and the psychiatrist's directions: don't wear black, don't cross your legs at the knee, don't talk with the tip of your tongue, don't walk on the tip of your toes, don't smoke with your fingers in a V, don't move your head, your eyes, your hips. I'd blubbered about the cure, sobbing maybe the shrink was right, maybe my mother was right, maybe I was wrong-handed, wrong-footed. And AIDS or not, maybe I had hell to pay.

The whole time I'd blubbered, Mercy had clicked and popped and sizzled her tongue. Yet she'd memorized the list and written it down. Through each don't, Mercy had drawn a red line then marked: Do!

"But I thought..." I started.

Mercy clapped the air with her hands. "Yes, *do*," she said. "Do this for me: be for yourself, mister sister. When you get out of this nest, hen-feather your rooster. Sissy everything you do. Mister everything you are. And when some damned fool tells you to stop fucking yourself to death, tell him you're fucking yourself awake. The world is a book if you only open your eyes to read."

Then she slipped one more item from the knot in her shirt-dress: a strand of black pearls. Each pearl glowed in her hands and together they looked like the beads from a rosary with the crucifix long lost to time.

"The only stories worth reading never end," she said. "Or else they all end the same way: To Be Continued. Your story is this: either you got lucky with a false positive or got unlucky with a bad blood test. So flip a coin and decide. Which way will you go? Heads or tails, whatever you choose, let it sound like thunder when you walk."

The next morning, I waited for Mercy to show as I sat with a zipper bag in my hands on the edge of the bed. I hooked my crucifix earring to the black pearls and folded the last page from a book into my empty wallet. The slim book was one of the first Mercy read, and the final words twisted into a paradox: "Soon, we will be again as we never were and endlessly are." The nonsense made my blood rise when she spoke it. Like a frustrated pupil, I wanted to wring meaning out of every word, to wrench a moral out of every sign. Yet Mercy made a joke of fake meaning, a farce of phony morals.

With only a few hours left until my noon release, I crossed the hall to find Mercy's room. The door was half-open, and when I pushed the knob, her bed came into view. The corners were neatly tucked, military style, with the pillow set on end, like a headstone. My throat tightened, and my tongue thickened. Where had she gone so early? Why hadn't she said goodbye? And how had she left: on a gurney or her own two feet?

When the fragrance of red berries and camphor filled my nose, I knew the answer. And when the floor buzzed with news of a missing patient and a missing nurse's uniform, I knew the story. Mercy had slipped out before dawn. She'd made it to the exit door before me. Now all I had to do was follow. It wasn't the end of anything. I wouldn't die of a scourge or a plague. A pulse beat in my wrist, the blood rushed to my chest. No one waited for me outside of Charity. My mother and father had never shown. My disco friends had never called. Yet I wouldn't walk out alone. I had Mercy's pearls now. Trust. Maybe there was nowhere to go, but it was morning, and there was everywhere to be. Once upon a time, I said to myself. It was a beginning.

AFTERWORD

DAWN CHORUS

When she enters the room she has them with her: flowers like bright crowns of light. Yet I look past them to her hands, clutching the bouquet as if she might wring mercy out of it. A haze surrounds her face and — for a moment — all sound is silenced. Even in the haze, that unreal bunch of roses and lilies shimmers in her hands with artful urgency. The paper and ribbon shine too, as if ripped from a still life on a wall. Her arrangement looks like a tribute for a ceremonial occasion, a birth or funeral, an occasion to reckon each breath as a temporary rite, each moment as a fleeting sacrament. My mother lays the flowers across my chest, and suddenly I look not like a patient on a hospital bed but a corpse in a sarcophagus.

The nurse from the hall looks in, tucks a chart under his arm, and says the last of the discharge papers can wait until noon. He also says that — in a way — I died, that the drug seizure briefly left me without air. I kept murmuring afterwards, but the words ran into a jumble. All except one. My lips came together to repeat my first word and the childhood nickname my mother gave me.

"Boo," I said, clear and strong.

As she props herself on the bed next to me, Mama remains silent at first, and I'm grateful. Too many words have passed between us already. We're far past apologies now, past repentance and atonement. Instead of talking, we stare at each other like strangers, and my fingers start to tremble and twitch. She runs her perfumed hands over my face, brushing away my unruly hair. Then, when her palm settles on my forehead, my nerves settle too.

Easy now, she speaks. Just two words: "Come home."

To a Cajun boy, that's not an invitation but a command. And I can see it: crossing the threshold with my mother, walking into the family den, slipping into my father's arms.

Yet I shake my head no — slowly — and meet my mother's eyes. Going back is no way to begin. In Louisiana, all roads lead to the gulf, and I've been in that black water too many times already.

Mama smiles. She knew I'd say no. She stands up, turns on her heels, and I hear it: the clink of a key on the counter.

"Yours," she says, "when you're ready, Boo."

After she goes, my chest shakes and my hands tremble again. Then I look on the counter a second time, and I see Mama left not a house key but a skeleton key. On the spine, there's an engraving in French. The words are a blur. Still, I take the skeleton key in my hand and stare at its secret. Maybe there's a door somewhere that fits the key. Maybe that door will lead to a library—or a church—filled with light. Or maybe not. Maybe it leads to no place at all. Either way, I know Mama means it as a sign. A key will lock or unlock, will let you in—or out.

Before I exit the room, I slip the key in my pocket, lie back on the bed and close my eyes with a song in my head. At the start, a slow and quiet melody, then a fast and furious rhythm, full of fiddles, accordions, and triangles. A Cajun waltz of loss and longing. A song of exile. Yet all the people in my head are dancing together as if celebrating at a fais do-do. Men with women, women with women, men with men. Pentecostal and Catholic. Sabine and Cajun. Black and white. *Tout ensemble.* Everyone whirling so fast that no one can tell the dancers from the dance. Their legs saw in and out to the beat. Their arms link and unlink. Then they throw back their heads, open their mouths to the heavens and let out a wild cry as I nod into a dreamless sleep.

When I wake, the clock strikes noon, the door cracks open, and the floor echoes with the sound of walking thunder.

Merci

Midwife: Stephen Kijak/DB
Den Mother: Eric Polito/Edie/Miss Bamboo
Little Sister: Jason Sellards/Jake Shears

Wild Boys: Andy Bailey/Iggy; Christopher De Kuiper/Stella;
Joe Marci/Little Joe

Souvenir

Makeup: Kevyn Aucoin/Glamour King
Hair: Newman Braud/Naomi Sims/Miss Gay USA
Photography: George Dureau/Master Valentine

Merci Encore

Samantha Shea & Georges Borchardt/Georges Borchardt
Literary Agency
Tyson Cornell, Julia Callahan, Alice Marsh-Elmer
& the whole flock/Rare Bird Books

The Antioch Review: "Flounder" & "Two-Headed Boy"
Epoch: "Revival Girl," "Wanted Man," "Skinwalker,"
"Feathers," & "Makeup"
Five Points: "Altar Boy"
Glimmer Train: "Father Fox," Finalist, Very Short Fiction Award
New Orleans Review: "Father Fox"
The Rattling Wall: "Masked Boy" & "Revelator"

National Endowment for the Arts